"We nee[...]

He folded his arms and [...] her. "We have nothing to discuss."

She kept her voice low. "I think we do. I remember when you were hunting Oscar Birch after he murdered his wife. I also found out that Oscar Birch recently escaped from prison."

"You're good at finding out facts. Must be an occupational hazard."

"Here's a fact that wasn't in the research. Oscar's the one who messed up your house, isn't he?"

"Could be."

She stepped closer to him, trying to capture his gaze with hers. "Bill...you've got to tell the police. You've got to get out of here."

"The cops know. They're after him."

"They'll catch him, surely."

Bill shrugged. "Could be."

She gaped. "You think they'll catch him, don't you?"

He stepped toward her. "I think that you need to stay away from here, from me, until this is all sorted out. I fixed your Jeep. Take it home and don't come back."

Books by Dana Mentink

Love Inspired Suspense

Killer Cargo
Flashover
Race to Rescue
Endless Night
Betrayal in the Badlands
Turbulence
Buried Truth

DANA MENTINK

lives in California with her family. Dana and her husband met doing a dinner theater production of *The Velveteen Rabbit*. In college, she competed in national speech and debate tournaments. Besides writing novels, Dana taste-tests for the National Food Lab and freelances for a local newspaper. In addition to her work with Love Inspired Books, she writes cozy mysteries for Barbour Books. Dana loves feedback from her readers. Contact her at www.danamentink.com.

BURIED TRUTH

DANA MENTINK

Love Inspired

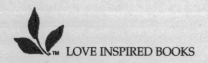

LOVE INSPIRED BOOKS

Recycling programs
for this product may
not exist in your area.

ISBN-13: 978-0-373-44454-0

BURIED TRUTH

Copyright © 2011 by Dana Mentink

www.LoveInspiredBooks.com

Printed in U.S.A.

Then Peter came and said to Him,
"Lord, how often shall my brother sin against me and
I forgive him? Up to seven times?"

Jesus said to him, "I do not say to you up to
seven times, but up to seventy times seven."

—*Matthew* 18:21–22

To my mother who has been there
every step of the way for all four of her girls.

ONE

The heat shimmered up from the asphalt as Bill Cloudman drove the pickup, Tank barking enthusiastically in the back. It had taken eight months away from Rockvale for him to realize he'd actually missed the ferocious heat. After two days back home, he felt as if he'd never left. This small town, snuggled up next to the Eagle Rock reservation, was undeniably a part of him, as much as he'd tried to escape it. He eased off the road that led away from his aunt Jean's dilapidated trailer, deep in reservation territory.

Aunt Jean was the reason he'd returned, her nasty fall the only thing that could draw him back to this place filled with bitter memories. Thankfully, she was recovering well, already back in her trailer making every guest feel welcome. Sharing a glass of iced tea and listening to her chatter had taken his mind off the past for a little while. Even though she was not his aunt by blood, he never thought of her as anything else. With her, he could pretend things were fine, that his sister, Leanne, was alive and they were a family, that his partner, Johnny Moon, hadn't been murdered.

That game got him only so far. Leanne was dead. Johnny was dead. No amount of wishing would bring them back again. His tension increased as he drove away, losing him-

self in acres of sunbaked trees and dry grass that surrounded him.

He breathed deeply as he drove the five miles to the small
home he'd left in the months following his partner's death. It
was remote, far from the nearest reservation neighbor, and he
liked it like that. Working as a Tribal Ranger, one of twelve
officers who protected life and property on the reservation
and surrounding areas, he'd appreciated the distance sometimes, the quiet. It had been a sanctuary—until Johnny was
killed. Then everywhere he looked he saw friends and neigh-
bors who knew how he'd let his partner die. Bill had packed
his bags and resolved never to come back—and he hadn't,
until Aunt Jean had her fall.

Bill exhaled slowly, trying to quell a sudden feeling of
unease. The tingle of alarm grew stronger even before he
crested the last ridge and his house came in sight. There was
an unfamiliar tang in the air, an odor that caused Tank to
growl as they crunched up the winding driveway.

Wrong.

Something was wrong.

He eased the truck to a stop, breath tight in his chest.

He got out and ordered Tank to stay. The dog barked his
displeasure, but obeyed.

Broken glass littered the ground, blazing in the sunlight.
All the front windows were fractured into bits except for sharp
teeth of glass that remained stubbornly in the frames.

Vandals with nothing better to do. Teens, he told himself.
Who else would cause such destruction?

Who else?

Muscles tight, he moved closer. A bucket of crimson paint
had been thrown at the walls. It stained the stucco like the
red spurt of blood. Angry, hateful.

The note was impaled to the wall by the blade of a knife,
plunged to the hilt into the wood.

Coming for you.

It needed no signature.

Oscar Birch's rage seeped through the scrawled letters.

Oscar, the man he had imprisoned.

The man who murdered his partner.

He didn't know how Oscar had wrecked his place when the man was supposed to be in jail, but he might as well have signed his name in the vicious smears of paint.

Paint that was still wet.

"You're not welcome here."

Bill Cloudman knew it, felt it, long before he found himself on Charlie Moon's gritty doormat two hours later. It had taken that long for his former colleagues to finish their investigation at his home and pass the information on to federal authorities. They told him the brutal truth with as much compassion as they could muster.

Oscar Birch had escaped.

The officers would try their best, but Bill knew with sickening certainty they would not capture the fugitive. Oscar was smart and wily and desired only one thing—Bill's death. Oscar wouldn't be captured or contained until he got what he was after.

Bill tried to focus on the hostile face of Johnny's uncle. "I came to warn you."

Charlie grunted. "Then you did what you set out to do."

Bill suddenly felt every one of his forty-five years weighing him down as he stood on the front porch of the small house, the South Dakota sun scorching through him with unrelenting fire. "And I wanted to see how you were doing. And Tina."

Charlie Moon raised a grizzled eyebrow. "Since you let her brother die?"

Bill exhaled. The words weren't unexpected, but they cut deep anyway. "I loved Johnny like a son, you know that."

"I don't know any such thing. I only know you were my nephew's senior officer. You were supposed to take care of him, watch his back." Charlie shook his head. "He was so proud when he joined the Tribal Rangers. So proud to work for *you*."

"I trained him the best way I knew how." Bill felt the surge of frustration that caused his voice to edge up a notch. With an effort, he kept it level. "It was a bust gone bad. Oscar knew we were coming."

Charlie's calloused fingers gripped the door frame, the pressure turning his knuckles white through the natural tan of his skin. "Words. Just words. Johnny went in first, a nineteen-year-old rookie—he went in first and got blown up. Can you tell me any of that ain't true?"

Bill looked at the red dust coating his boots. "No."

"And can you stand there and say to me it wasn't your fault? You've been a Tribal Ranger for what? Twenty years? And a rookie walks in after a fugitive first, without waiting for a backup team? That how it's supposed to go, Bill?"

He could not answer against the thickening of his throat.

Charlie looked at him, lips in a tight line. "If you came back to Rockvale for forgiveness, you're not going to find it here. Not with me. Maybe not from anybody."

A six-year-old girl with a thick braid of black hair peeked past Charlie. "Hiya, Uncle Bill. Have you come back?"

Bill knelt and blinked back an unexpected wash of tears. "Hey there, Tina. I've missed you."

"Me, too," she said. "I got the birthday card you sent and I put the stickers on my lunch box. Where's your dog?"

He nodded toward the massive rottweiler watching their every move from the back of the truck. "Right over there."

"Can I play with him? I want to see if he's learned to fetch."

Bill was about to answer when Charlie pulled the girl back.

"Mr. Cloudman is not your uncle and he's leaving now. He can't play with you anymore."

Tina shot her uncle a puzzled look. "Never?"

Charlie nodded grimly. "Never."

"Is it 'cuz Johnny went to heaven?"

Charlie patted her shoulder. "We'll talk about it later. Go back to your room and put your books in order."

"But Uncle—"

"Go," Charlie said, voice hard.

Tina's face was puzzled as she wiggled her fingers at Bill before she disappeared into the house.

Bill straightened. "Is she…how is she doing?"

"Better than you'd think for someone who lost her mother to cancer and her big brother to murder. 'Course, Johnny was more like her father, him being so much older and since her father took off before she was born. So all she's got left is her old uncle Charlie and this piece of wasteland." He gestured to the horizon, harsh cliffs painted against the setting sun. "How's that gonna get her any kind of future?"

Images of a previous sunset flashed through Bill's brain. The explosion, the ferocious hatred of the man bent on killing them. The ease with which Oscar Birch had been able to murder Bill's partner. And now the murderer was back with a different target in his sights. Bill looked up to find Charlie staring at him.

"Heard you helped bust Oscar's son near the Badlands."

"Yeah." He'd gone to assist his friend Logan to keep Oscar's son, Autie, from killing a woman named Isabel Ling. They'd gotten Autie, all right, and remanded him into custody. In the process Logan had found his soul mate in the strong-willed Isabel. At least there was a silver lining—for Logan anyway. The guy deserved it. Charlie's voice intruded on Bill's thoughts.

"Heard Oscar's son died."

"Yes." Autie had finally run out of luck. He'd made a break for it on his way to prison and been felled by a volley of police fire. Bill had felt nothing when he heard, no grief, no satisfaction; just the same numbness that had taken hold of him since the afternoon Johnny Moon was killed. He hooked his thumbs in his belt and let his gaze wander to his boots again.

Charlie's laugh was harsh. "That's justice, I guess. Oscar killed Johnny. You killed his kid. Now he knows something about my pain."

Though Bill said nothing, he knew Charlie was wrong, dead wrong. Oscar was filled with hate and anger that sizzled hotter than the Dakota desert, an incendiary rage that would not be satisfied or dulled by grief. And he was here. He might even be watching right now. Bill felt a chill in spite of the heat.

A bark from the bed of the truck pulled Bill from his thoughts. He noticed the curtain move in the front window of the small house. Tina was still watching. He tried to make his expression more pleasant. "Anyway, I thought you should know Oscar's escaped."

The old man wiped a hand over his mouth. "Listen, I got enough problems. Not my job to help you catch him again."

"I wasn't asking for your help. I'm not a Tribal Ranger anymore. I just wanted to tell you and see if you or Tina needed anything."

"She needs her big brother, but you can't give her that, can you?"

The door swung shut, the sharp click loud in the stifling air.

Bill put his palm to the wood, warm from the late afternoon heat. *If I could have that minute back, Johnny would be alive.*

The curtain fluttered again and Tina's little face peeked out. She mouthed something, a gap showing where she'd lost a tooth in the time he'd been away. Her expression so resembled her brother's that he was momentarily frozen. He forced a smile and walked down the drive, the enormous mass of a child's lost innocence weighing him down.

Heather Fernandes heaved a sigh. The guard at the entrance to the massive underground research facility, DUSEL, looked down at her, no expression on his stern face except for the slight uplift of one thick eyebrow.

She straightened, the steering wheel hot, since she'd turned off the air to prevent the Jeep from overheating. It was already making strange noises and she couldn't afford a repair bill. "All I want to do is talk to Dr. Egan. I've called dozens of times and gotten no response. I'm a reporter with the *Desert Blaze*."

She didn't entirely blame Egan. In his position, she wouldn't speak to reporters, either, especially not hacks for a local rag that was mostly filled with ads for used trucks and prickly pear jam. Egan was used to being interviewed by respected science magazines, like the kind she'd worked for in the past. "I used to write for *Horizons in Science*."

His eyes flickered as he took in her beat-up Jeep. "And I used to guard Buckingham Palace. This is just my summer job."

It wouldn't do any good to prove she was telling the truth. She gritted her teeth and looked past him as the dying sunlight painted the distant cliffs. Somewhere, concealed by construction equipment and the dip and swell of brown-covered hills, was the deepest mine in North America. Only, now the goal was no longer hauling out gold, but building the finest Deep Underground Science and Engineering Laboratory in the world. The best of the best, the most cutting-edge science so close, yet it might as well be on the moon. "Here's my number. Please have Dr. Egan call me."

She snapped out her business card and reversed the Jeep, suspecting the guard was laughing as he returned to his air-conditioned post.

Laughing that a seasoned forty-three-year-old reporter was so easily defeated? Or amused that Heather actually claimed she had written for *Horizons?* She groaned. If it weren't for the framed copies of long-ago articles, she might have believed it was a joke herself. Now she was reduced to writing a piece about some piddly fossil find and covering the local town events. She eased the Jeep down the road a couple of miles, rounded a corner and pulled over to the shoulder. Turning off the engine, she sipped some iced tea out of the thermos and considered. In years prior, her *Horizons* press pass had given her access to anybody, anywhere. The who's who in the science world practically salivated for the chance to air their discoveries in the magazine.

She recalled a time when she thought Rockvale might even become a home to her. She remembered a trip a year and a half before to this town, when she and Bill Cloudman had struck up a friendship. Her cheeks warmed. More than a friendship, on her side anyway. But things had ended badly after six months. Very badly. Shame licked at her insides again.

She'd decided to return to her father's house in this nowhere town a week ago only after she'd learned that Bill had gone, checked out from the world after the murder of his partner. Where was he now?

It was probably good for him to have left. Maybe he'd found a new life. She shifted uncomfortably on the seat, remembering the emotion that had shimmered in his dark eyes the day he'd arrested her. There might have been love there, but she'd seen only betrayal, the same kind of betrayal she'd lived with since her mother had walked away from Heather and her father when Heather was just a child. Walked away. The only written contact she'd ever made was that one brief note.

I read your lagerstätte article. Excellent and well re-searched. You should be proud. Mother

The insanity of it still boggled Heather. Her mother had chosen to break her silence and comment about some ancient set of fish fossils buried in remote Montana?

She'd wanted to scream at the injustice of it. *What about me? Aren't you interested in me? Your child?*

But even more unsettling was how much Heather had been moved by that one word.

Proud.

Why should that one word coming from her mother, the stranger, the betrayer, the woman she should hate, mean so much?

Heather flopped her head back on the cracked vinyl. Would her mother be proud now? Proud despite her daughter's battle with alcoholism? Losing her job and relationship in one fell swoop?

When she felt the despair creep up again, she grabbed hold of her lifeline.

God, thanks for giving me the strength to stay sober.

It wasn't eloquent or lovely, but she figured God was used to her constant stream of thankfulness mixed in with regular pleas for help. True, she hadn't gotten her job at *Horizons* back and there was no hope that she would ever understand her mother's abandonment, but she was sober and God got all the credit for that gigantic achievement.

Restlessly she twisted her long mane of curls into a messy braid. It didn't do much to cool her, but at least it kept her hands almost as busy as her mind. Her phone rang and she snatched it up. Maybe Dr. Egan had decided to speak with her after all.

"Good afternoon, Ms. Hernandes."

The unfamiliar voice was gravelly and low, tinged with a slight drawl.

"Hello. Who am I speaking with?"

"A friend. I have a story you will be most interested in, I'm sure."

She frowned and pressed the phone closer to hear.

"Who did you say you are?"

"I didn't, but you will be hearing from me soon."

"I don't talk to people unless they identify themselves." She tried for a strong tone, in spite of a tickle of unease in her stomach. "Who is this, please?"

A harsh laugh filled her ear. "We have not had the pleasure of meeting. Yet."

She sat up straighter. "Identify yourself or I'm hanging up."

"Such rudeness doesn't become you." More laughter. "And your braid does not flatter, Ms. Hernandes. You should keep your hair loose."

The phone disconnected.

Her body erupted in prickles of fear. She cranked on the engine and locked the doors. Breath coming in panicky bursts, she careened off down the road. No one in the rearview. No one following behind. Should she call the police? Remembering her DWI arrest, she knew she did not want to have anything to do with law enforcement again.

Calm down. Think.

Who was the guy anyway? His voice was unfamiliar. Probably just a crank caller.

But he'd been watching her.

She took a deep breath, starting violently when the phone

rang again. After another look in the rearview, she pulled over. This time she checked the number and kept the engine running. With trembling fingers she answered, relieved when her editor's voice boomed over the line.

"Some vandalism up at Bill Cloudman's property. Need you to check it out and write it up."

At the mention of Bill's name, Heather felt an odd tightening in her stomach. "Isn't there anyone else who can do it?"

"Just one person and that's you. Go take a picture before it gets dark. And add a bit to the webpage about it."

"But..."

He'd already hung up.

Heather disconnected. Vandalism wasn't exactly a riveting subject and Bill's property had been abandoned so long it was the perfect target for teenagers with nothing else to do. It was also remote.

The stranger's voice whispered through her memory.

We have not had the pleasure of meeting.

Yet.

She considered calling someone to go along with her, but there was no one she could think of. Steeling her spine and saying another quick prayer, she drove along, ignoring the now-familiar knocking from her engine.

Her phone remained silent for the rest of the drive. The road sloped upward, twining through stands of trees. Every small movement drew her attention, every dart of a lizard on the shoulder made her jump.

"It was just a crazy crank caller, Heather. Relax and do your job before you lose this one, too."

As the miles ticked by, she realized for the first time how utterly remote this little corner of South Dakota was. Acres of dry grass and rock-strewn hills, with not a soul to be seen anywhere.

Gritting her teeth, she continued on.

When she finally pulled onto Bill's property a half hour later, her mouth dropped open. She wasn't sure which shocked her more, the bloodred paint defacing the house, or the sight of Bill Cloudman, his dark eyes filled with thunder, staring right at her.

TWO

Heather tried to plaster what she hoped was a professional look on her face. "I...I didn't know you were here."

"Didn't see a need to alert the press." His face was expressionless, but his eyes kindled with emotion. "Aunt Jean told me you moved back and got a job with the paper." He looked away. "I guess you didn't get any of my calls or emails."

She felt a rush of shame. Maybe she should have handled things differently, but their last encounter was a messy tangle of humiliation and she'd wanted no part in reliving it then. Or now. Best to keep things professional. "I was told to come and write up the vandalism. Any ideas who messed up your property?"

He shook his head. "No, and I don't want it in the paper."

A big black dog charged out from the trees and raced over, immediately rolling over at Heather's feet. She scratched his smooth belly. "Hello, Tank. Glad to be home?" She looked again at the garish paint. "It looks recent. Is somebody trying to tell you something?"

He folded his arms across his chest. "It's not important. Don't you have a bigger story to cover?"

A bigger story? She flushed. Not anymore. Maybe not ever. "No, I don't."

He blinked and looked away at the sun as it melted into the horizon. "There's no story here," he said in a softer tone.

As much as she wanted to get right back into her car and drive away, she knew she had to face this moment, to stand straight and hold on to the new, stronger person she'd become. "I think there is, and I've been assigned to write it up." She took out her camera and aimed it at the paint.

He stepped in front of her, broad chest blocking her view.

She glared at him. "One picture?"

His lips tightened, but he didn't move, muscled arms folded across his front.

"Thanks anyway." She would not beg. She'd done that before and her own cowardly pleas still rang in her ears. If he would not cooperate, at least she could leave. She wrenched open the Jeep door and jammed the key in the ignition. It took a few moments before she realized the engine was not cooperating. After two more tries, she slammed a hand on the steering wheel. "Piece of junk," she muttered.

Bill walked to her window. "I'll give you a ride home."

"No, thanks." Riding next to him? Sitting beside the strong, silent man from whom she had run like a wounded animal? It was too much to bear. She shouldered her bag and got out. "I'll walk."

He sighed. "I'm going to have to follow you in the truck to make sure you get home, and it's gonna take all night."

"I can get home okay, Bill." She felt flustered, embarrassed to be floundering in front of him, of all people. "I'm…I'm not the same person I was before." She didn't understand her need to tell him that she'd grown up, overcome her addiction. Most of all she hated the slight wobble in her own voice. Why should he believe her? Sometimes she didn't even believe herself.

"It's too long a walk and too remote an area." He walked to his truck and opened the passenger side. "Get in."

Forcing herself to take a breath, she tried to think rationally. He was right—it would take her hours to walk home and the strange phone call still bothered her. Surely she could handle sitting next to Bill Cloudman for the drive. It wasn't as if the man would bore her with small talk. Just a few miles and it would be over. She looked into his dark eyes.

"All right," she said. With as much dignity as she could muster, she got in. "If it's not too much trouble."

Bill grunted and took off at a good pace, but twice she caught him peering in the rearview mirror.

"Looking for something?"

"No."

"So you really have no idea who trashed your house?"

He gave a noncommittal shrug. She shot him a stealthy look. There was a sprinkling of silver in his dark hair and he looked tired, more tired than she'd ever seen him. His broad shoulders seemed to carry some tension. She had the sudden urge to speak, in spite of herself.

"I heard about Johnny. I'm sorry."

He blinked and the corners of his mouth softened for a moment. "Thanks. Me, too."

She should have called him, sent a note at least, but she hadn't had the courage. Her own weakness pained her.

They lapsed into an uncomfortable silence. She was again struck by how much had changed in the time they'd been apart. She remembered riding in that very seat beside him, exploring the incredible landscape—until everything fell apart. The pain and humiliation of their last meeting rose up as strong as ever.

She'd begged and pleaded. *Just let me go. I promise I'll never drive drunk again.*

He'd looked at her with eyes full of tenderness as he'd arrested her anyway.

The thought made her squirm and the truck seemed to slow to a snail's pace.

The sun set into a pool of fire as they drove back to Rockvale, followed by the appearance of a sliver of moon in a shroud of clouds that hinted at a summer storm. He turned off the main road and eased the truck along a twisted gravel path that served as the driveway to her father's house. Perched on ten acres of land, it would be his retirement getaway.

If he ever can retire, she thought, feeling an uncomfortable squeezing in her gut. She'd cost him so much and he'd bailed her out so many times at his own expense. Sonny Fernandes would never admit it, but saving his daughter by paying for a treatment program and legal fees had wiped out any chance that he could enjoy his golden years anytime soon. She felt the stab of guilt again as she pictured him supervising a construction crew building a bridge somewhere in California.

Soon, Heather. You'll prove yourself again so you can pay him back. All she needed was a story that would lift her out of anonymity and, if she was patient, Dr. Egan might be just the source—if he would trust her enough to give her access to a lab story. Her editor would have to run it, even though it wasn't her beat.

She sighed as they drove past a pile of tangled branches. In the meantime, she would work on fixing up her father's place. Not a glamorous job, but a work of love.

Bill pulled to a stop and Heather grabbed at her bag. In her haste she upended the purse, spilling the contents onto the floor. With clumsy fingers she shoveled the things back in and practically ran for the porch, calling out as she went, "Thanks for the ride."

She let herself into the house with a surge of relief. She'd made it through the trip without saying something stupid—or worse, crying. It was over. The scrabble of paws on the floor announced Choo Choo, a graying Labrador mix. He lumbered up and presented himself for petting.

"Hello, baby. Did you miss me?" She got him a small chunk of boiled chicken from the fridge, which wouldn't be too hard on his old teeth, and kissed his head. "Mama needs a shower, Choo Choo. You wouldn't believe the day I've had."

She did her best to wash away thoughts of Bill and her sorry excuse for a career. Wrapped in a light robe and relaxed for what seemed like the first time that day, she padded barefoot into the kitchen for a glass of iced tea, gazing out the window into the darkened landscape. Her father's property and that of his neighbor Charlie Moon were not actually on reservation land, but their acres mingled with Eagle Rock reservation in a seamless expanse of plateaus and gorges.

In the distant rocky canyon that divided her property from Moon's, a light flicked on and off. She froze. Whoever was moving around had no business there, unless it was Charlie himself doing some night hiking.

Not likely, as he had a bum foot and a small child to take care of. It was impossible to tell if the intruder was actually on her property or Charlie's, but one thing she knew for sure— whoever it was didn't belong there.

She threw on some clothes, and grabbed her father's rifle and a flashlight.

Choo Choo looked hopefully up at her.

"You need to stay here this time. I'll be back soon," she said, hurriedly pulling the door closed behind her.

Making her way as quickly as she could, sticking to the cover of the massive pines that clung to the rocks on either side of the canyon, she pushed forward, keeping the trespasser's bobbing flashlight in view. Several times she had to stop and catch her breath, waiting for the gleam of light to show again.

Finally the light stopped and a softer, steadier glow took its place. A lantern. The intruder must have fixed on a spot to explore. She felt a sudden reckless anger surge through her. This place was entrusted to her, the only thing her father owned free and clear, and this person, whoever it was, was probably out looking for fossils to steal and sell on the black market. Or maybe it was some teens bent on finding a place to party. Didn't matter. She was going to make sure they left and never came back.

"Hey, down there," she yelled. Her voice rang through the quiet. "You're trespassing on private property. You need to get out of here right now."

The light was extinguished. She waited a moment to listen for the sounds of scuffling feet, but there were none. Flicking on her own flashlight, she beamed it down into the gorge.

A shot rang out, whistling past her head. She jerked back behind the tree for cover and readied her own weapon, heart hammering in her chest. Another shot sizzled by. From a crouched position she aimed the rifle high. Hopefully a warning shot would be enough to show the intruder who he was dealing with and convince him to leave.

She squeezed off a round. The report of the rifle deafened her. By the time she raised the weapon to fire again, a dark shape rose from behind the clump of nearby rocks and hurtled on top of her. The gun flew from her grasp and sailed through the air. She rolled and tumbled, the attacker still holding on to her. Her hair fell across her face and she couldn't get a look at the man, but his arms were like iron straps as they held her fast. She felt a calloused palm over her mouth before she could suck in enough breath to scream.

"Quiet," Bill Cloudman grunted in her face, "or whoever that is will kill us both."

* * *

Bill kept his hand over her mouth until he was sure she wouldn't scream and give their location away. When he eased his hand aside, he whispered a warning. "No more noise."

He got to his feet, staying low behind a massive granite boulder, and tried to listen for sounds of movement. Heather scrambled up next to him.

"What are you doing here?" she whispered.

He pulled something from his pocket and handed it to her. "You dropped your phone in the truck. Came back to return it and I saw somebody on your property. Thought I'd check it out, until Annie Oakley came out with guns drawn and the shooting match started."

"Hilarious, Bill." She pressed closer to his back. "Who's out there?"

He ignored the prickle on his neck where she spoke into his ear, the clean scent of shampoo that clung to her hair. "Not sure." If it was Oscar, then it was time to settle things, and he didn't want her anywhere close by. "I am going to go down there and see if whoever it was is holed up. Go back to the house and lock the door."

She was about to answer when something streaked by their legs. "Choo Choo. Come back here," she hissed. "I must not have closed the door all the way. I've got to get my dog." She moved forward and he grabbed at her arm.

"Go inside."

"I'm not going to let him get hurt."

"It's just a dog."

She shook him off. "Like Tank is just a dog?"

He bit back a comment, wondering how she'd managed to best him already. She was smart, more than smart, a fact he'd known the moment she'd arrived in town the first time. He felt the warring desires to draw close and keep her at arm's length. In the past, he'd struggled between the two compulsions, got right to the brink of letting down his defenses, and then he'd arrested her for drunk driving and that was the end of anything they might have had. Maybe someday he would be able to tell her why he hadn't shown mercy in spite of her pleas. Someday. But right now was not the time.

Heather retrieved her rifle and moved along a ridge of rock before stopping to turn back to him.

Bill resisted the urge to hoist her over his shoulder and hogtie her. Instead he hurried to catch up as she moved farther away. At least he could try to prevent her getting shot. If the shooter really was Oscar... He shook away the notion. *Deal with the situation as you would any other, Cloudman.*

He caught up with her when she stopped to peek over the top of a hunk of granite.

They stood silently, their breaths the only sound.

He strained to see any sign of movement or spark of light.

Nothing.

"They must have gone," Heather whispered, her damp curls brushing his cheek. "Choo Choo is probably hiding around here somewhere."

Bill shook his head. "I'm going to take the trail down to the bottom. Don't follow or you might get hurt. If there's trouble, call for help."

"But what about...?"

"If your dog is down there, I'll bring him back." Without waiting for an answer, he drew his weapon and moved down the dark slope between two massive walls of stone. The strange insulating quality of being enveloped in rock awed him, as it had since he was a little boy, scrambling through South Dakota's labyrinthine trails. He'd always felt most at home deep in some stone passage with no people nearby, yet still surrounded by the hidden crush of life that filled every pore of this place. His aunt Jean used to chuckle at him and say, "Why do you think God made those cliffs so high, Billy? Because He wanted you to look up."

Tonight the isolation held a tone of menace. He slowed his pace, listening for the slightest noise or movement. The far-off whine of a coyote floated through the canyon, answered by a yowl from the other side. The gunshots hadn't scared them away any more than had the locals' determined efforts to dissuade them from eating their chickens. Coyotes were persistent.

He grimaced, thinking of someone else who fit that description. Crazy woman, almost got herself killed waving that rifle around. That bravado could be deadly. Didn't she realize what she was walking into?

No, she didn't. And he didn't know for sure, either. Not until he got a visual.

Breath controlled, body inching along in painful slow motion, Bill pressed on.

He eased around another pinnacle of rock, feet as silent as he could make them on the red earth. He flicked on a penlight. A partial shoe print caught his attention, pressed into the dry powder of the path. He bent to look closer. An athletic shoe, worn, from the look of the impression. The air seemed to thicken around him.

Farther along he caught a tire impression, small and narrow, blurred in the dirt along the trail. He waited until a cloud passed over the slice of moon before he moved closer.

Even as he crept around the corner, he knew he was not alone. Was it instinct or was his subconscious hearing what his ears could not? Didn't matter. The feeling that had kept him alive for an entire career hummed in his body. He took a deep breath. "Give it up, whoever you are."

The stillness was split by the sound of a dirt bike revving to life. Bill had time to press himself against the rock wall as a helmeted figure on the churning motorbike shot forward, gripping the handlebars with one hand and swinging a short-handled shovel with the other.

The shovel caught Bill in the shoulder, cutting through his shirt and into the muscle, spinning him off balance.

He rolled out of the way, tried to aim and found the bike already vanishing down the rock passage.

Pounding footsteps echoed through the canyon and Bill knew it was Heather before she ran into view.

Her mouth rounded into an O when she saw him. "Are you okay? Who was it? Did they hurt you? What happened?"

He straightened, a lance of pain arcing across his shoulder. "Too many questions."

She huffed. "Well...take them in order, then. Are you okay?"

Pulling a hand away from his shoulder, he saw that his fingers were bloody. "Mostly. Good news is he got me with a shovel."

"Who? How is that good news?"

"Wasn't a gun and the shovel seems to indicate he was just a fossil hunter."

"*Just* a fossil hunter?" She fisted her hands on her hips. "Last I heard, stealing fossils from private land is a crime and taking them from public land is a felony. And they shot at me, remember?"

"Shots were meant to scare you, not kill you."

"Well, that's comforting. At least I found Choo Choo. I put him back in the house."

The exasperation on her face almost made him smile as he holstered his weapon. "Got to get a call in to the cops. You're not on reservation property, but it wouldn't hurt to let the Tribal Rangers know, too," he said, taking out his phone as he started up the trail. She sighed loudly and fell in behind him.

"Bill," Heather whispered, dogging his heels, "why do I get the feeling you aren't telling me everything?"

He finished talking to dispatch and clipped the phone to his belt. "You heard every word of that call. Maybe your career makes you paranoid."

"And maybe you're trying to cover something up." She squeezed in on the path next to him. "Why didn't you want to talk about the vandalism?"

"Just didn't." He felt her eyes on him and he quickened his pace. "I'll see you home. Captain Richmond will meet us there to take statements."

He pushed on until they reached the small wood-sided cabin. He scanned the windows for any sign of movement, more out of habit than concern. Maybe Heather didn't live alone; maybe she'd gotten married or something. He had to shake his head at that notion. Who would have the fortitude to try to corral an unpredictable creature like Heather? He'd come close, he'd thought, and that had ended in disaster. A vivid picture of his grandfather Mel sprang into his head, working with a massive wild mare crazed by a piece of barbed wire wrapped around her foreleg.

He'd stood there for hours, just watching, talking low and soft to that animal when she'd come close. Bill could still hear the frantic pounding of the hooves, the enormous body thrashing inches from his grandfather. The moment she went still, Grandpa Mel removed the wire with one swift snip of his cutters before he'd let her free to find her herd. The horse had looked at them both for one long moment before she thundered away and Bill thought he'd never seen anything so beautiful in his life. He wondered why looking at Heather brought up the old memory.

Heather pushed past Bill and opened the door. She left it ajar, so he figured she meant him to follow. Then again, she might just as easily slam the door in his face. Though he'd rather pull out his teeth one by one than admit it, the severing of their relationship had cut him to the core and now the disequilibrium he felt at having her near rolled around inside him. He stood uncertainly on the porch until she called from inside.

"Are you coming in, or what?"

Feeling as if he was about to step in front of Grandpa's wild horse, he squared his shoulders and walked inside.

THREE

Heather left Bill to find his way and went directly to the back bedroom. Choo Choo rose stiffly, tail arcing like a pendulum, and trotted over. She sank to her knees. "Hey, boy." She rubbed his face, muzzle gray-white against the black of his fur. "Were you scared from the gunshots? No more escaping. Let's get you some food, huh?"

The dog gave her a lick and lumbered down the hallway. Bill looked up when they entered.

"Didn't know you had a dog."

"He's new. Got him in Miami."

Bill arched an eyebrow. "Doesn't look new."

"Okay, so he's not exactly new." She sailed past him into the kitchen and warmed some rice and chicken, which Choo Choo lapped eagerly. In truth, Choo Choo was supposedly twelve years old, according to the owner who'd kept him locked in a cement pen with no shade and sometimes no water. Heather would never admit to Bill or anyone else that she'd sold her television and paid the guy five hundred dollars to take possession of Choo Choo.

Choo Choo looked at Heather with filmy eyes as if he read her thoughts.

New or not, you're worth every penny, sweetness.

Returning to the living room, she found Bill holding his

shoulder with one hand and peering at a square of limestone with a delicate imprint of a fern, perched on a shelf.

"You into fossil collecting now?"

"No. That was my mother's. I found a box of her things in the closet."

She took a first aid kit off of the shelf and wet a towel. "Sit down and let's get this over with."

He looked at her, ink-black eyes expressionless. "It can wait."

"I don't want blood on my floor."

He considered for a moment before he sat at the butcher-block table and peeled up his sleeve.

She hesitated and finally handed him the damp towel. No need to go all Florence Nightingale on a man who would rather be anywhere else. He took it and wiped the blood off his shoulder, then swabbed the wound with the antiseptic she provided.

She handed him a square of gauze, which he held in place while she taped it to his dusky skin. The muscles were hard and unyielding under her fingers.

Bill sat without complaint, his eyes examining the bookshelf next to the table and the picture of a serious woman with the same dark hair as Heather.

"Do you ever hear from her?" he asked softly.

Heather picked up the first aid supplies. "No."

When she looked at him again, she saw the ghost of a smile on his mouth.

"Is something funny?" she asked. "A guy shoots at us, you get creamed with a shovel and something is funny?"

"Ironic, more like. You don't like to answer questions, but you make a living prying into other people's lives."

Her cheeks warmed. "I make my living asking questions, not answering them. So here's one for you. What is really going on? It seemed like you were expecting to find something entirely different than a fossil hunter. And I think you know perfectly well who vandalized your house, don't you? Are you going to answer any of those questions?"

He sat back in the chair and pursed his lips in thought. After a moment he shook his head. "No."

She groaned. Choo Choo scurried in, confusion in his filmy eyes. She called to him and rubbed his ears until he sank to the floor in a black mound of contentment. Bill had walled her off and she knew that she'd given him plenty of reason to do so. "You're even more stubborn than you were before—" It was too late to undo the damage. *Before Johnny was killed.*

An almost imperceptible tightening of Bill's lips made her realize she'd said exactly the wrong thing.

He didn't reply and the silence extended into the uncomfortable zone. She squirmed in the chair trying to think of something to say to break the awkward quiet. A knock on the door startled her.

Captain Richmond stood on the step, his khaki uniform sweat stained and wrinkled. The bags under his eyes seemed to accentuate his droopy appearance. His mustache twitched as he spoke. Next to him was a dark-skinned man in a Tribal Ranger uniform. Heather recognized him as Al Crow, a friend of Bill's.

"You called about a trespasser?" Richmond said.

"Heard the call. Thought I'd come, too," Crow said.

She showed them in. Crow took in the sight of Bill and his bandaged arm, and his thick brows rose in concern.

"Okay there, man?"

Bill nodded and shook hands with him and Richmond. "Glad to see you."

Richmond cleared his throat. "Yeah. Heard you were back. Thinking about signing on with Tribal Rangers again?"

Heather saw Bill's gaze falter for a moment. "No." Bill stood and rolled down his ruined sleeve. "I'm retired."

Richmond nodded slowly. "So give us the rundown."

Bill spoke, with a few interjected comments from Heather, while the officer scribbled in his battered notebook.

"Sounds like some kids," Crow said. "They're always looking for things to do. Doesn't come across like a big deal to me."

"I'll take a better look in the morning," Richmond said.

"I'll come, too," Crow put in.

"Not your jurisdiction, Ranger," Bill said with a smile.

Crow held up his hands and laughed. "No problem to help out a badge brother."

Richmond nodded. "Good night, Ms. Fernandes." He turned to Bill and jerked his head toward the porch. Bill followed him and Crow outside.

Heather itched to know what they were talking about. As she casually walked by the window on her way to the kitchen, she could not see the expression on Bill's face, but Richmond's brows were drawn together, his face dead serious. Crow's arms were folded across his barrel of a chest, his gaze fastened on his boots. Heather slid open the tiny window above the sink. No reason not to catch the cool night breeze. She washed her hands and put the kettle on to boil, straining to catch bits of the conversation. Still the two men talked, until Bill held up a hand and took a step away.

She caught Richmond's parting words to Bill as the men walked into the darkness, the captain's hand on Bill's shoulder.

"Watch your back, Bill. We don't want any more murders."

Heather watched them go, the shrill cry of the kettle mingling with the strange worry deep in her gut.

* * *

Heather woke late the next morning to Choo Choo's snoring. She padded to the kitchen, pondering all the while. Why was Bill Cloudman prowling properties at night? And why was she worried? Bill could take care of himself. Her instincts continued to prickle until she could stand it no longer. With toast in one hand, she picked up the phone with the other.

The clerical person at the Tribal Ranger office was coolly efficient.

"No, Bill Cloudman is not consulting with the Tribal Rangers."

"Not even in an unofficial capacity?"

"No, ma'am."

Heather disconnected and pulled up an archived article on her laptop about the Johnny Moon slaying.

Tribal Ranger John Moon was killed yesterday by a bomb reportedly rigged by suspected killer Oscar Birch, who was holed up in a cave just outside Badlands National Park. Upon entering the cave, Moon triggered an explosive attached to a trip wire and was killed instantly. Birch escaped, while Tribal Detective Bill Cloudman, who was also on scene, attempted to resuscitate Moon. Birch was later captured at a roadblock ten miles from the site of the incident and taken into custody.

The article went on with further details and a "no comment" from Bill Cloudman.

Heather sighed. Bill didn't want to comment on anything as far as she was concerned. Whatever closeness she'd felt between them before her arrest was gone. Choo Choo finished his breakfast while Heather paced the small front room. Though Bill's strange behavior continued to prey on her mind, she had more practical matters to attend to. Until she retrieved her car from Bill's place and had it fixed, she was going to have to work from home.

It took only a moment to add a line to the "latest buzz" section of the *Desert Blaze* website about the vandalism at Bill's place. Her editor wouldn't be pleased that there was no accompanying photo, but hopefully it would appease Bill. She added another entry about the upcoming church pancake breakfast and signed off before focusing on the print articles that required her attention.

She needed to write a piece on a minor fossil find by week's end. She'd put it off for a while because it was on Bill Cloudman's adopted aunt Jean's property. Heather had met the amazing woman before things fell apart, and deep down, she felt ashamed at having to face her. There was also the story about the abandoned uranium pit a resident had been complaining about for years. It had the smell of a real story about it. After a phone call to leave a message with the man who'd reported the uranium pit, Heather found her attention wandering again.

"A little fresh air couldn't hurt." Pocketing her phone, she grabbed the dog's leash. "Let's go for a walk, Choo." They headed into the glare of morning sunlight. The summer heat still surprised her every day, even though she'd lived in South Dakota for a few years as a little girl. Maybe she'd been too preoccupied then, wondering if her mother, Margot, would embrace the new beginning her father had intended for them. She hadn't, and Margot's dissatisfaction with her life and her health had only worsened.

Heather wiped at her face. Not even noon, and the temperatures were scorching. Tattered clouds seemed to press the heat back down at her, taunting her with the promise of a cooling rain. As she passed her mailbox at the end of the drive, she saw a note wedged underneath the red flag.

From the cops? She didn't think so. Maybe Dr. Egan had

changed his mind about the lab article. Snatching it, she read the ink scrawl.

I'll give you the real story on Bill Cloudman.

Her fingers turned to ice. The real story? She remembered the strange phone call from the day before.

Choo Choo pulled on the leash, so Heather stuffed the letter into her pocket and followed, but her mind was alive with questions. Who had written the message and what was his connection to Bill Cloudman?

It took a few minutes of walking before she worked her way to the other side of the issue. A stranger had been on her property again, someone not willing to sign the note and leave a contact number.

Her instincts prickled like exposed wires. She made up her mind to talk to the police, in spite of her reluctance to show her face at the station again.

She and Choo Choo stuck to the shaded perimeter of the trail that led from her house down toward the canyon where the ruckus had occurred the night before. There was no sign of movement now except for an eagle soaring in lazy circles above her. The rocks sloughed away in rivers of red and gold, dotted with clumps of needlegrass and the flicker of color from some late-blooming monkshood. Choo Choo nosed along as they walked and Heather found herself moving toward the old timber bridge that spanned a low spot in the canyon, connecting her property to Charlie Moon's.

She stopped to pour some water from a bottle into her cupped palm for the dog, who slurped it up and gave her a lick on the cheek to boot before wagging his tail at a little girl who seemed to appear from nowhere. It took Heather a moment to identify the child as Tina Moon, Johnny Moon's sister. Her dark hair was pulled back in a messy ponytail, several thick strands that had escaped the elastic hanging in her eyes.

"Hiya," she said. "You used to be Uncle Bill's girlfriend." She bent to pat Choo Choo.

Heather felt her cheeks go hot. "Oh, I, um, know Bill, yes. He, er, used to be a friend of mine."

Tina shoved her hands into the pockets of her jean shorts. "Not anymore?"

Heather found the girl's dark stare unnerving. "Have you seen your uncle Bill since he got back?"

"Uncle Charlie said Uncle Bill's not my uncle anymore." She sighed, fiddling with a compact she pulled from her pocket. Heather hid her smile as the girl looked into the tiny mirror and puckered her lips. Tina put the compact away and eyed Choo Choo. "Your dog is real slow. Not like Tank. Anyway, I gotta go. I'm not supposed to be playing here."

"Why not?"

"Uncle Charlie said there's a monster on the loose and he'd be real mad if he knew I was out here instead of inside playing. Bye." She gave Choo Choo a final pat and trotted off, leaving Heather in a cloud of confusion.

A monster? Maybe it was a story Charlie told to keep Tina from wandering, but the few times Heather had seen Tina in the past, the child was always on her own as she meandered around the property and her guardian had never seemed to mind before.

Then again, things might have changed since Johnny was murdered.

She thought of Bill Cloudman's strange behavior. He preoccupied, closemouthed, as if he, too, was on the lookout for a monster.

On her way back over the bridge, she pulled out her satellite phone and accessed the internet, typing "Oscar Birch" in the search window. It took only a moment before her suspicion was confirmed.

In spite of the radiant heat, Heather went cold inside.

Tina was right. There was a monster on the loose.

Bill stood in the relative cool of his front porch that afternoon, wiping oil off his hands from fixing Heather's Jeep. Tank shifted uneasily at his feet, waiting for a ball to be thrown or the jangle of truck keys. He let out a bark, which elicited only a distracted look from his owner, lost in the memory of a long-ago sun-scorched day.

Then, too, he'd had the tight feeling in the pit of his stomach, a prickle of instinct that told him something was going to go wrong. On that afternoon there had been a similar cover of clouds that undulated across the sky. Difference was, he hadn't been alone then. Johnny Moon was there, chatting away, eager as always for any kind of excitement, reminding Bill in some ways of Bill's dead sister, Leanne.

"You got to let go sometimes, Sarge," Johnny would say. "Live a little. Ask that fine reporter out. You know she's got it bad for you."

He smiled at the memory. He'd decided to follow his partner's advice and ask Heather to dinner that same night. Yes, Johnny had been full to the brim with life, even though Bill sensed worry in his young partner in the months before his death. Something was distracting him, but it never for a moment took away his ebullience.

The trip wire did that.

A thin filament of death, set carefully in place by a man as lethal as a rattlesnake with a bite every bit as vicious.

Bill would go to his grave believing Oscar had known they were coming, planned the execution down to the last detail. Only, Oscar hadn't known Johnny would cross it first.

And neither had Bill.

He sighed, watching a raccoon waddle down the thick bark of a pine tree on his way to forage. Tank jerked alert at the sound and took off running for the critter, which about-faced and climbed back up, hissing and snapping his displeasure at the dog.

Bill's mind wandered back to Heather and her geriatric pet. The presence of a dog in her life amused him. She acted tough, but he'd seen glimmers of that soft spot in her before. He couldn't reconcile the two opposites in his mind, so he stopped trying. It was one of the many things he'd probably never understand about her.

A dull ache was settling into his upper arm and he flexed his injured shoulder. Fixing the Jeep, after spending most of the morning cleaning up the broken glass, hadn't helped the wound. Mopping up the paint had proved mostly futile, but he'd done what he could. The house was still smeared in ugly streaks of red.

He lingered there on the porch a long time, until the sun was high. He allowed himself to remember, for the briefest of moments, how much his sister, Leanne, had loved the sunshine. Years before, he might have summoned up a prayer for those he had lost, Leanne and Johnny. Instead he turned back inside the paint-spattered house to find his gun.

When the Glock was cleaned and oiled, he holstered it to his side, and after he fed Tank, they headed out onto the property. It was a sprawling ten acres of parched flatland, rolling hills and a spring, hidden by a thick cluster of pines. The smell of it soothed him—rusty earth, dry grass and heat. He'd been gone for so long, the ground had lost some of its familiarity. He needed to reacquaint himself, to relearn every dip, every hollow, every possible shaded nook that had grown over in the time he'd been away. His survival might depend on it.

Bill started hiking to the farthest edge of the property where it sloped downward into a dry wash. The boulders piled in crazy formations along the edge formed a labyrinth of rock and hence a myriad of hiding places. As far as he could tell by a careful examination, no one had been prowling there anytime recently. The dry soil was marked only by the curving slices of rattlesnake tracks and the scattered dry bones of a hare that had probably fallen victim to a coyote.

He continued upslope to the pine grove, a welcome cool against the sun that was hammering down mercilessly. Tank took advantage of the shade to stretch out and put his bony head on his paws. Here again, there was no sign that any trespassers had been present. Bill removed a pair of binoculars from his backpack and scanned the area below, his defaced cabin, tucked up against the side of a granite cliff, the flat area surrounding it and the distant cliffs standing like broadchested sentries against the sky. Nothing out of the ordinary until Tank sat up abruptly, ears swiveling, body rigid.

"What do you hear, Tank?" Bill whispered.

Tank listened for another moment before he took off, bounding down the trail and disappearing into the trees. Bill followed as quickly as he dared, keeping to the shadows as much as possible.

His pulse pounded in his neck. Was it Oscar?

He stopped behind a fallen trunk and watched.

Tank was not visible but he heard a quick bark, just one, and then the property fell into silence again. Bill had seen Tank in attack mode before only a few times, one of which involved a massive, drunk dirt biker who'd caught Bill unawares and knocked him to the ground. The dog had leaped immediately into the fray and caught the biker's biceps between his jaws, which clamped viselike until Bill scrambled to his feet and called off the animal in stern Lakota, the language in which he'd trained the dog. It had taken all of Bill's powers of persuasion to convince Tank to let go of the whimpering bad guy.

Unfortunately, Tank's impulsivity often got the better of

his training. Had he gone after an animal? Or encountered a creature with much more deadly potential? Bill took a few deep breaths to relax his muscles before he slid the Glock from its holster and ran to the next tree.

Tank let out a whine. Bill couldn't see the dog through the thick screen of towering pine. Inching closer, he took each footstep gently, easing his boots into the soft cover of pine needles.

Closer now. There was a small movement ahead. He took a breath and prepared to step around the wide trunk. Forcing himself to keep breathing, he did a slow count to three and charged.

FOUR

Heather screamed as Bill Cloudman suddenly leaped from behind a tree, gun in hand. Tina looked up from her kneeling position scratching Tank's belly.

"Hiya, Uncle Bill."

Bill's face blanched slightly under the dark skin and he immediately pulled the gun behind his back. "Tina. What are you doing here?" He gave Heather an incredulous look. "Did you bring her?"

Heather swallowed hard and tried to find her voice, heart still hammering against her ribs. "No, I didn't. I was on my way to talk to you and I found her walking a couple miles outside town. It didn't seem safe to let her walk on the road alone, so I gave her a ride."

She caught the question on his face. "I rode my dad's old motorcycle. It's parked over there in the shade."

Bill looked from Heather to Tina. He got down on one knee and gently caught her chin on his finger until her gaze met his. "Did your uncle give you permission to come?"

Tina shrugged.

He raised an eyebrow, his face stern. "Tina?"

Tina shook her head. "Uncle Charlie doesn't want me to talk to you anymore now that Johnny's dead, but I wanted to come and see you and Tank. I liked it when we played fetch.

I thought he could help me hunt for fossils. Look at this one." She held up a curved bit of white that she fished from her pocket.

Heather saw a stain of emotion wash over Bill's face before it was hidden behind his stoic mask. "Never mind that now. You should not have left without telling your uncle. He's probably worried about you. Come back to the house and I'll call him."

Tina rose and Tank trotted at her heels as they returned to the cabin. Heather was unsure if she should tag along or not until Bill called over his shoulder, "Thanks for taking care of her."

Heather took it as an invitation and scurried to catch up with him. "No problem. We need to talk, Bill."

"No, we don't."

She bit back an impatient retort. Their past aside, she needed to confirm her terrible suspicion. "Yes, we do. I know what's going on."

He ignored her and quickened his pace. Heather was practically running by the time they reached his cabin. Tina scrambled inside after Tank, and Bill stopped abruptly on the porch. "Appreciate your help. I'll handle things from here."

She reached ahead of him and pulled the door closed. He turned on her, the muscles of his jaw twitching. She'd seen that intensity in him before and it made her shiver.

"I've got to take care of Tina now," he said.

"No, you need to talk to me."

He folded his arms and glowered at her. "We have nothing to discuss."

She kept her voice low. "I think we do. I remember when you were hunting Oscar Birch after he murdered his wife."

Bill stared at her, but didn't answer.

She forced her way through the awkward silence. "Oscar killed Hazel and he was on the run."

His jaw clenched, but he still did not speak.

"He was still at large when I...left." She added softly, "And then he killed your partner."

"Correct. That's old news." His eyes wandered over her face. "A lot of things have changed since you went away."

She swallowed. "You helped capture Oscar's son, who died on the way to prison."

That comment elicited a blink from Bill. She pressed on. "I also found out that Oscar Birch recently escaped custody."

He folded his arms. "You're good at finding out facts. Must be an occupational hazard."

"Here's a fact that wasn't in the research. Oscar's the one who messed up your house, isn't he?"

"Could be."

She thought suddenly about the note on her mailbox, the strange phone call. A shiver of fear coursed through her body, leaving her cold. "Bill, I need the truth."

"That's something, isn't it?" His eyes blazed. "You didn't need anything from me a while back. Didn't even need to return my messages. Now you come here *needing* the truth."

She wanted to scream. "I'm not talking about you and me or what happened. I'm talking about right here and right now." She stepped closer to him, trying to capture his gaze with hers. "Oscar blames you for the death of his son. Has he returned to Rockvale to kill you?"

Bill looked steadily at her this time, eyes black bright and glittering with an intense emotion. "I certainly hope so. Oscar hasn't learned his lesson."

Heather's mouth fell open. "Bill...you've got to tell the police. You've got to get out of here."

After a moment he turned abruptly and went into the house. She followed in a daze, watching while he poured two glasses of water and handed one to her. "Cops know. They're after him. Local guys and the Feds."

She took the water and gulped some down. "That's good, then. They'll catch him, surely."

Bill drained his glass and set it on the table. "Could be."

She gaped. "You think they'll catch him, don't you?"

He took the glass from her hand. "I think that you and Tina need to stay away from here, from me, until this is all sorted out. I fixed your Jeep. Take Tina home and don't come back here. I'll tell Charlie you're on your way. I'll bring your motorcycle back soon."

"Bill..." She put a hand on his arm, but he pulled away. A flash of some emotion rippled across his face. Maybe it was the lingering hurt at the way she'd shut him out after the arrest. Perhaps it was the disappointment of having let his guard down with a woman who turned out to be an alcoholic.

Her eyes wandered over the tile counter, to a red-checkered cookbook, the same one she had jokingly given him before her disgrace.

You need to learn to cook, she'd said with a laugh.

Now that I've got someone to cook for besides the dog, maybe I will.

She remembered his laugh, the sparkle in his eyes. The sight of that cookbook brought back all the shameful choices she'd made, the ways she'd tried to hide her addiction from him.

She wanted to tell him about the phone call she'd received. About the note. But she saw the coldness in his eyes and the ferocious desire to avenge his partner's death. Bill was right. She should stay out of his life.

She would go to the police and let them handle it.

"Tina," she called to the girl, who was busily twining a thread around Tank's collar. "Let's go home. We can ride in my Jeep."

Tina looked up. "I liked riding the motorcycle."

"Me, too, but the Jeep will have to do this time. Come on. Uncle Bill wants us to go."

Heather felt Bill's eyes on her as she walked Tina outside, but she did not look back.

Once was enough.

Bill called Charlie and explained things.

"I told her she was to stay inside," Charlie sputtered.

"She's a kid. She made a mistake."

Charlie hung up, leaving Bill to hope the little girl wouldn't be punished too severely. This time he agreed with Charlie. With Oscar on the loose, it was better for everyone to stay away from him, including Tina.

And Heather.

He was surprised that seeing her brought up such a mess of feelings for him. He'd thought after losing Leanne, her and then Johnny, he didn't have feelings left. He was wrong. His gut was a jumble of anger and longing. He pictured her brown eyes, remembered the feel of her hand on his arm.

Let go of that, Bill. Remember the anger. Feed it. And find Oscar.

He went outside and rolled Heather's motorcycle into the back of his truck. The sooner he delivered it and severed all connection with her again, the better. His phone rang as he closed the tailgate.

The voice of Tribal Ranger Al Crow was heavy with excitement. "Bill? That you?"

"What's up, Al?"

"I knew you'd want to be in on it. We got him."

Bill's gut tightened. "What?"

"Oscar. Got a tip he was holing up in an old camper by Swallow Cliffs. Moving in on him now. Want in?"

"Oh, yes," Bill said. "I want in."

* * *

Swallow Cliffs was the local nickname for acres of prairie grassland nestled up to a dry streambed that cut along the bottom of a cliff face. Spring rains would transform the area into a vigorous river, which provided plenty of bugs and fresh water for the hordes of swallows that nested in the cliff walls. Now, as Bill and the three other men watched through binoculars from behind a screen of shrubs, the only movement came from the sudden dive of a bird and the swish of dry grass tickled by the hot wind.

Next to Bill, Al Crow and Captain Richmond peered through binoculars. The camper perched crookedly in the grass was rusty, the windows obscured by blinds. Jim Rudley, the same federal investigator who had assisted in the manhunt for Oscar after Johnny's death, held a phone to his ear. Crow shifted uneasily. "Could handle it ourselves."

Richmond grunted. "He's calling for the bomb squad, just in case this is an ambush."

Both men shot a look at Bill. He could remember the blast so clearly, the one that had killed Johnny. The flash, the explosion that had made his ears ring. Holding his partner's hand and begging him not to die. He forced a steady voice. "Who tipped us?"

"Reggie," Crow said.

Reggie was a mechanic who did any odd job he could find on the Eagle Rock reservation. He'd proven to be a help to the Tribal Rangers on many occasions.

Crow continued. "Said kids were using the trailer for drinking and such a while back, so he keeps a close eye on it. Saw some tracks near the creek, saw a light last night and called it in to us this morning."

Bill stared at the trailer. It had been there so long, on an abandoned stretch of land, he could no longer remember who had left it there. Nothing moved in the interior. Nothing that he could see, anyway.

Richmond and Crow stood next to him, hands on their guns, tense. He knew they felt the same mixture of anger and excitement that he did. If Oscar was in there, they could put away the guy who killed Johnny. This time for good.

Rudley clicked off his phone and nodded to Bill. "Explosives guys are on their way, but it will be a while."

Bill looked again at the rusty trailer.

I'm coming for you.

Oscar was a twisted man, incapable of normal emotions, his troubles probably born of the days he lived with his mother and a steady stream of abusive men, according to the sketchy facts collected about his life. As far as Bill knew, Oscar loved only two things—his mother, who had passed away two decades before, and his son, Autie, now dead after trying to escape arrest.

It did not matter that it was not Bill's finger on the trigger. In Oscar's mind Bill had murdered his son. This was not about laws or justice. It was revenge, pure and simple, and Bill hungered for it just as much as Oscar.

The feeling shamed him. He knew what Aunt Jean would say.

Leave the judgment to the Lord, Bill.

Well, the Lord had abdicated the day he let Johnny get blown up.

Without a word, Bill drew his weapon and headed for the trailer.

Behind him he heard Crow gasp.

"Cloudman," Rudley whispered. "Get back here."

Keeping to the edge of the foliage as best he could, Bill crept on toward the trailer.

Rudley tried to catch him. "Don't be stupid. You can't fix what happened by getting yourself killed."

But Bill had already left the shelter of the branches and begun running toward the trailer, head low and moving as fast as he dared.

He reached the trailer and plastered himself against the side, listening, the heat from the metal soaking into his skin. No sound. No movement. Edging closer to the tiny window, he noticed a gap in the blinds that would enable him to get a look inside.

Inching along, he saw in his peripheral vision that the other officers had moved in closer to provide backup. They were good men who would die trying to help him even though he was not one of them anymore.

No one is going in there but me.

He would not allow anyone else to die.

Pulling even with the window, he took a deep breath and popped his head up to get a look. All he saw was the darkened interior, no sign of anybody lying in wait.

He eased back to the front door, checking carefully on the ground for any signs that it was rigged to explode, though he knew his checking likely didn't matter. Oscar was a genius with all things mechanical or explosive, so he wouldn't leave any telltale signs if he'd wired the door.

Bill eyed the ramshackle structure again, noting another window on the far end, over the hitch. With the other officers closing in, Bill headed for it, climbing up on the tow hitch and risking another look inside. Still no sign of life. Resisting a sudden urge to pray, instead he turned his gun and brought the butt down on the glass.

It shattered, cascading in jagged shards down to the dusty ground. He didn't wait any longer. Plunging feet first through the window, he hit the floor and crouched, gun ready.

But there was no one. Perfect silence except for the tinkle of the glass that continued to drop onto the worn linoleum floor. Oscar wasn't here. Bill felt it even before he did a quick search of the small bedroom area and the even smaller bathroom. No one. The tip was wrong. He would not be bringing Oscar Birch down today.

Could be that Oscar had never even been here in the first place. Bill ground his teeth.

He heard shouts from outside.

"Cloudman?" Crow yelled.

Bill checked the door from the inside before opening it. "All clear."

As the officers piled into the trailer, Bill's eye was caught by an envelope lying on the kitchen table. He approached warily, but the envelope had not been rigged to explode. Bill slid the contents out.

"Cloudman," Rudley snapped, face red with exertion and anger. "That was crazy. You endangered your life for nothing after I specifically ordered you to wait."

Bill's eyes locked on the photos in his hands.

Rudley spoke louder. "I guess you need reminding that you're not an officer anymore. You got no badge and no business interfering. We informed you as a courtesy and you blew it." He stepped forward. "Are you listening to me, Cloudman?"

But Bill was not listening. His fingers were suddenly cold, the icy feeling flowing up his arms and into his heart.

He shoved the photos back into the envelope. "We've got to find Heather. Now."

FIVE

Heather sighed as she drove away from Charlie's house after dropping Tina back home, accepting an awkward thank-you from Charlie before he closed the door in her face. Tina had shot Heather one last look from the window and Heather had almost laughed out loud. The expression on her face told the story. She was going to get in trouble, but she had enjoyed the adventure to the fullest. It took Heather's mind off her worries for a moment, but the memory of Bill's grim face remained.

She phoned the police department and learned that Captain Richmond was out on assignment, so she left a message for him to call. A couple hours and many errands later, with the Jeep air-conditioning running at full tilt, she retrieved a message from her editor assigning her a story about the upcoming fair on the reservation. She wrote down the pertinent details with a sigh before she turned the phone to silent as she guided the Jeep back out to the DUSEL.

Her life was falling to pieces, or so it felt. She'd returned to this place only to find Bill Cloudman was back. Now he was engaged in some bizarre game of cat and mouse with a deranged killer. He wanted her out of his life and that seemed like a good plan, except that she couldn't seem to shake him from her mind.

Do your job. Get your career back. Leave Bill to take care of himself.

Recalling the only picture she'd seen of Oscar Birch in the articles she'd found, eyes glittering from under a shroud of grizzled beard and long hair, she shivered.

Lord, please watch over Bill.

She checked her watch. Four o'clock. Nearly quitting time. Pulling up the road and peering toward the lab, she could see Egan's silver Lexus stopped at the guard gate, checking out for the day. Finally, luck was on her side. An inside scoop article with Dr. Egan was the key to getting her career as a science writer back. Besides, they'd met before, so she had an in, sort of. But he was refusing to talk with her, so she'd have to take more drastic measures.

She pushed the Jeep ahead and sped over the peak and down the winding road before pulling to an abrupt stop where the walls of red rock squeezed in together, leaving just enough room for two cars to pass.

Easing the Jeep into the middle of the road and hoping that no other traffic would ruin her plan, she stopped and turned on the hazard lights. The temperature in the vehicle rose with each passing minute, until her long brunette hair was damp with sweat.

The Lexus moved around the turn and she watched in her rearview as Dr. Egan stiffened, taking in the Jeep stalled on the road. She waved a hand out the window and he pulled to a stop. He climbed out, dressed casually in jeans and a plaid shirt that pulled tight over his expanse of stomach, his graying beard and long sideburns at odds with the shining dome of his bald head.

"I'll call for road service," he said as he walked toward her Jeep.

"No need." Heather got out quickly and approached him. "I just want to talk to you, Dr. Egan."

"Who…?" he said, alarm written on his face.

She held up a reassuring hand. "Heather Fernandes. I'm a reporter."

His eyes narrowed a moment and he rubbed his beard with the antenna of his phone.

"You used to write for *Horizons*. You interviewed me quite some time ago about…what was it?"

"Wind erosion and climate change."

"Ah, yes. You are a friend of Bill Cloudman's."

She started. "You know Bill?"

His face grew pained. "Actually, I knew his late sister, too."

Bill had never shared the particulars of his sister's death with Heather, only that she'd died much too young, at age fifty-six, months before Heather came to Rockvale, and it grieved Bill deeply. Though she wanted to ask Egan about it, she feared losing her momentum. "I need your help for an article."

He looked away and then back at her. "Ms. Fernandes, perhaps I can save us some time. The reason I haven't returned your phone calls is that I'm aware you no longer work for *Horizons* magazine."

She swallowed. "How did you know that?"

"A simple internet search. I usually look into the reputations of people who want interviews with me." He sighed. "That sounds arrogant, but the fact is reporters seem to enjoy stirring the pot and I need to be able to trust my interviewers."

Heather opened her mouth to argue, but the twinkle in his eye stopped her. "Dr. Egan, you're right. I don't work for *Horizons* anymore and I'm sure you know why. Long story short is I blew it. I'm sober now, and I'm looking to restore my credibility. I write for the *Desert Blaze* until I can make that happen. A behind-the-scenes interview with you about the lab would go a long way toward giving me my career back."

He smiled. "Good for you. Owning up to your mistakes takes gumption. And I would like to help you do that if I could, but the fact of the matter is we are not allowed to discuss lab operations. Your editor will understand, I'm sure. You can talk to our PR person if you need something in particular."

He walked back to his car.

Her voice cracked as she called to him. "Actually, the big lab story is my idea." She added hastily, "but with your cooperation, I'm sure my editor would let me write it. For now, I've been assigned some smaller pieces and I wanted to get some quotes from you."

He paused. "I really am sorry, Ms. Fernandes."

She felt the desperation rise, as if her last chance was about to slip away. She had to get him to work with her on some topic, anything. "I've been working on some notes about uranium poisoning. Lots of exposed pit mines in the area. You could contribute your expertise." *And then we can talk about the lab when I've earned back your trust.*

He shook his head. "I admire your persistence, but I'm not interested."

She pulled out the big guns. "How about fossils? There's been a find south of town. I'm working on that story, too."

Dr. Egan turned back. His brow wrinkled and then he burst into laughter. "So I guess you did your homework. You know I'm really a paleontologist at heart."

Heather smiled. "I remembered from my *Horizons* research that it's a passion of yours."

He slid on a pair of sunglasses and opened the car door. "Tell you what. If that fossil find turns out to be anything interesting, you call me up. That's a subject I don't mind talking about."

She eased the Jeep to the side of the road and let him pass. It wasn't what she wanted, but it was a start. Heather drove home with more hope than she'd felt in a long while. The fossil story was going to be her in with Dr. Egan, an opportunity to show him she could be trusted so he'd allow her an interview about the lab.

One chance. One shot at writing a serious piece was all she needed. It might not get her hired back at *Horizons*, but it would be a step toward redemption. Resisting the urge to break the speed limit, she made her way home, noting that whatever Bill had done to the engine seemed to have fixed the strange knocking from under the hood.

A quick stop at home to check on Choo Choo, and Heather would be on her way to the police station to fill them in on the strange phone call and note. A flicker of fear tightened her stomach for a moment before she forced it away.

Leave the worry to the cops. They will know how to handle it.

The temperature still hovered in the triple digits as Heather pulled up the drive to her father's cabin. Though it meant a formidable electric bill, she left the air conditioner running to keep things pleasant for Choo Choo while she was gone. That dog was the best listener of any living creature she'd encountered and he'd sat with her through her tears, despair and prayers for her sobriety. Heather knew that the old Labrador was a God-given blessing. The least she could do in return was keep him from overheating.

She noticed it the minute she crested the driveway. The gate. The old wooden gate was ajar.

Throwing open the car door, she leaped out.

"Choo Choo?" she yelled. "Where are you?" She'd installed a dog door to give Choo Choo access to the backyard while she was away. If he'd gotten out…

She ran into the yard and did a quick scan. No dog.

Back to the front and she unlocked the door with shaking fingers. Maybe the dog was inside, enjoying the cool.

"Choo?" she yelled again, but there was no noise of scrabbling nails on the hardwood floor.

She looked at her watch. She'd been gone for several hours. The dog could be anywhere. Fighting a surge of panic, she raced outside again and shouted for him. The sound echoed along the sunbaked ground and down into the canyon, but there was no answering bark.

In a misery of uncertainty, Heather turned in helpless circles, trying to decide which direction to start the search. The rugged canyon? Along the brush-lined road that led back to the highway? It was ferociously hot. Choo Choo would never find his way home on his own.

Tears threatened as she imagined the old dog desperately searching for her through his blurred eyes.

She ran back to the Jeep, and her fingers were just grasping the handle when a voice called.

"This your dog, ma'am?"

She jerked around to find a short mail carrier, holding a U.S. Postal Service sack with one hand, his other wrapped around Choo Choo's collar.

With a cry of joy, Heather ran to the dog, who nearly knocked himself over with his own whirling tail.

"Oh, Choo. I was so worried." She buried her face in his fur, momentarily unable to speak.

The man's face creased into a smile as he took off his cap and wiped his brow. "Saw him back on the main road, sniffing around. Figured he had to belong here."

"Thank you so much for returning him. It was so kind of you."

He waved a hand. "No problem." He eyed the house behind her. "You should get a better lock for that gate, ma'am."

Heather shook her head. "That's the weird thing. It has a good latch. I was sure it was closed tight when I left."

He chuckled. "Not tight enough to keep this old boy in."

She sighed. "You're right. Listen, I really appreciate you walking him home, especially in this heat. Won't you come in for a drink of water?"

The little man shook his head, settling his cap onto his balding head. "Gotta finish my route," he said, blue eyes twinkling. "Nothing will stop this guy from doing his duty. Might as well give you your mail while I'm here." He handed her a stack of envelopes.

Heather watched him walk back down the long drive before she took Choo Choo back in the house.

If the mailman hadn't found him...

She shuddered, pouring the dog a fresh bowl of water before going outside to check the gate again.

I'm sure it was closed when I left. It might be nothing, her own carelessness.

Or it might not.

Back inside, shivering, she made up her mind to head to the police station immediately, and this time she was taking Choo Choo with her. The roaring of multiple engines brought her to the window. She watched, mouth open, as a police car pulled to a stop, followed by a Tribal Ranger's vehicle.

Most surprising of all was the arrival of Bill Cloudman in his truck, his face a grim mask.

He hurtled out, leaving the truck door open as he strode to the front door.

"Heather?" he hollered, louder than he'd meant. "Are you in there?"

Crow and Rudley caught up, Rudley's face still flushed with anger.

"This is not..." Rudley began.

Bill wasn't listening. He drew his weapon and the officers stepped to the side of the door as they heard the sound of someone approaching.

Heather opened it, eyes wide at the sight of them.

He exhaled, releasing the weighty terror that had filled him on the drive over.

"What's going on? You look like you're ready to break down my door," she said, her glance darting from him to the other men and back to him.

"Are you alone?" he barked.

"No," Heather said. "Choo Choo's here, too." The dog pushed by her leg and wagged his tail at them. After a moment of hesitation, she added, "Do you all want to come in?"

He wanted to say an emphatic no. His insides were on fire, shot full of emotions that nearly floored him with their intensity. After long months of being numb, he did not like the sensation. He joined the others in holstering their weapons and followed them in. Heather beckoned them to sit on the worn sofa and provided glasses of ice water. Bill chose instead to stand. "Why didn't you answer your cell? I called a half dozen times."

She raised an eyebrow at his tone. "I put it on silent and forgot about it. Why?"

After a warning look from the FBI agent, Bill left Rudley to introduce himself and do the talking before he said something he shouldn't.

"Miss Fernandes, have you had any contact with a stranger recently? Any threats or situations that seemed odd or out of place?"

Bill was dumbfounded when she nodded.

"I got a phone call and a note." She provided the details.

Bill felt as if his blood had started to boil in his veins. "Where's your phone?" He took it from her and scrolled through her call list, writing down all the numbers on the notebook Crow handed him.

Rudley took the note she retrieved from the kitchen drawer. "It's him, all right. He didn't even bother to disguise his handwriting."

"Who?" Heather stared at them. "Do you think the call and note are from Oscar Birch?"

Rudley nodded. Bill noted that Heather didn't look altogether surprised. He rounded on her. "So you had a note and a call from this lunatic and you didn't think that was something to share?"

"I meant to share it. That's why I made an appointment with the police, but you all beat me to the punch."

He saw the flash of anger, the tightening of her full lips.

"You should have told me."

She glared. "You ordered me to leave you alone, remember?"

"That was different."

She fixed him with a look. "What's changed? Why are you here now?"

Bill looked down for a moment to try to gain some control. "We got a tip and went after him. He wasn't there, but he left this." He slid out the envelope and handed it to her.

She took it, fingers brushing his. As she removed the photos, the color drained from her face. "They're…they're pictures of me."

One of her talking to Bill in front of his vandalized house, hands on hips, another holding his arm, a beseeching look on her face.

"Yes," Rudley said grimly. "We believe he's targeting people close to Bill, to make him pay for Autie's death. Toying with them to get to Bill."

She blinked. "But we're not…I'm not…"

Crow cleared his throat. "Oscar lived in Rockvale for a

long time. He must have known that you and Bill were…together before."

Bill saw the heightened color in her cheeks. Their past was a chapter they both wanted to close, but it seemed Oscar had reopened it for them.

She sat heavily in a wooden chair. "This is ridiculous. I'm here to earn a living, that's all. I have nothing to do with Bill anymore."

She didn't look at him, but he felt the words cut into his heart. Why? he wondered idly. She'd been out of his life for a long time. Why did it still hurt?

Brushing the feelings aside, he moved closer. "You need to leave Rockvale. Go back to Miami. Anywhere, as long as it's not South Dakota."

Her head shot up, a look of defiance on her face. She waved the pictures. "This isn't my problem, remember? You're going to handle it all and I'm to stay out of it. I can do that, live my life, do my job and stay away from any odd strangers."

"No," he all but yelled. "You don't know this guy. He's crazy and he enjoys inflicting pain. He'll worm his way into your life until he has you where he wants you and then…"

Rudley held up a hand. "Miss Fernandes, though Bill is *not*—" he stressed the word "—in a law enforcement role anymore, I think in this case he's correct. It would be better for you to leave. Oscar isn't going anywhere until he gets what he wants here in Rockvale, so it would be safer for you to go elsewhere."

Heather squirmed on the chair. "I'll need to think about it."

Rudley nodded. "Fair enough." He stood, Crow rising along with him. "I've got a few phone calls to make, but I'll step outside and give you some breathing room."

She nodded, still not looking at Bill. He wanted to take her arm, pull her away and make her promise to get on the next plane out. The last thing he needed was for something to happen to her.

Rudley handed Heather a small photo as he exited. "Here's the most current picture we have of Oscar Birch." He continued out into the brilliant sunshine, Crow just behind him. Bill was about to leave as well when he heard a strange cry.

He turned to find Heather openmouthed, a look of horror on her face, picture clasped between her trembling fingers.

He went to her. "What? What is it?"

"This man…" she whispered, the photo slipping from her fingers to the floor.

"Oscar?" He could hear her breath coming in little gasps. "Tell me, Heather."

"This man," she started again. "He's the mailman."

SIX

She finished packing the next morning. One of the advantages to living below the poverty line for months was she didn't have many belongings. The horror still coursed around her body. Oscar Birch. She'd stood face-to-face with the pleasant, round-cheeked man who happened to be a cold-blooded killer.

The police surmised Birch had staged Choo Choo's escape and subsequent return, wearing a postal uniform he'd lifted from somewhere. But why? Why go to the trouble? Just to terrorize her?

No, she thought grimly. To terrorize Bill.

To hurt him.

To send the message that Oscar could get to the people Bill cared about.

She zipped the suitcase closed. Oscar had made a mistake there. She and Bill might as well be strangers to each other. Bill was not acting out of love, merely protectiveness and the all-consuming need to defeat Oscar, the man who killed Johnny.

The feel of Oscar's calloused fingers as he'd returned the dog remained on her skin. She'd actually invited the man in for a drink of water. He could have killed Choo Choo, or her, for that matter. Or he could have put a letter bomb in the mail that the police had confiscated; the man was an explosives expert, after all.

His words came back to her.

Nothing will stop this guy from doing his duty.

She sighed. Her departure came at a bad time—she knew she might never get another chance at a story about the DUSEL. Plus she really had nowhere to go, no job waiting. She hadn't resigned from the *Blaze* yet, figuring she could at least finish out her stories long-distance until the month's end. Then there was the matter of her insufficient means to rent an apartment. She could ask her father for money, but she'd rather go hungry than take any more of his hard-earned paychecks.

When the tingle of panic started up again, she said a string of silent prayers until it died away. God would help her survive. He would never forsake her. He'd proven that when she'd been at her lowest moment, afraid to trust herself or anyone else.

She looked out the window and saw Bill slouched in the front seat of his truck. He'd been there all night and she suspected he'd remain fastened to her like a shadow until she left South Dakota for good.

She felt a pang at leaving him, just as she had when she'd run with her tail between her legs months ago. Deep down, it was a relief to leave, to be forced away from any more possible encounters. A relief…and cowardice.

It was running away.

And she felt ashamed at her own eagerness to do so.

Bill's presence in the truck spurred her on. There was no choice but to leave the crazy Oscar Birch behind and pray that Bill could capture him before he exacted his terrible revenge. She called to Choo Choo, and with one last look around the tidy cabin, she left, locking the door behind her.

Bill got out of the truck and walked over to her Jeep. "Got everything?"

She nodded.

He hesitated, shifting his weight from foot to foot. "I'm sorry it had to come to this, but it's the best thing. We both know that."

Was he really sorry to see her go? She looked at his eyes, which he abruptly swiveled away from her. There was a profound relief in his face that shone through the carefully controlled expression. He was pleased that she was leaving, and the notion pained her.

"Where are you headed?"

She managed a smile. "Miami. I don't think Choo Choo will like being put in a crate, but he's a pretty good traveler. I'll leave the car here until it's safe to come and get it." She eyed the cabin. "I hate to leave it here empty. I'm not sure when my father will be coming back."

"I'll keep an eye on it for you." He loaded her suitcase into his truck and let Choo Choo in the front seat.

"Do you think you'll catch him?"

His mouth tightened. "I'll catch him."

The chill in his words cut through to her core. "I hope you do, Bill. I..." She reached a hand toward him, wanting to touch that warm, brown skin. Instead she let it fall away.

I'm sorry that I ruined things with us.

The words wouldn't come out. She could tell that he wouldn't welcome them anyway. All he wanted was for her to leave Rockvale for good.

Swallowing the bitter taste in her mouth, she climbed into the passenger seat. Choo Choo gave her a lick and settled himself between her and Bill. They drove into a spectacular blaze of sunrise and headed toward the main road.

Heather remembered that she'd turned off her phone the

day before. She reached into her bag and flipped it on. The screen indicated she had a voice mail.

Oscar?

Stomach tightening, she clicked on it.

Static crackled through the line, peppered with her father's voice.

Honey...sorry I wasn't home...know it will...hard but I am asking you to take care of...I'll be home when I can. Call you soon...battery's dying. Love you.

She felt a surge of joy at hearing from her father, but the message confounded her. She played it again.

Take care of what? What was he talking about?

There were no other new messages on her phone.

Bill gave her a puzzled look but did not comment.

She pressed her dad's number. Ten rings and it went to voice mail.

"Dad, it's Heather. I'm flying out of Rockvale today. I couldn't understand your message. Call me back." She hung up. "Weird."

Bill raised an eyebrow. "Your father?"

"Yes. He wants me to take care of something, but I didn't get the gist of it."

"Whatever it is, call me and I'll handle it for you."

He would, too. She glanced at his serious profile, the weathered face that didn't smile often, but lit up when it did. He didn't laugh often, either, but in the last few weeks of their time together, he'd seemed happier than she'd ever seen him. She wouldn't forget the moment he'd opened her cookbook present and thumbed through the pages as if they contained the secrets of the universe. Shame closed in on her again.

Why hadn't she been able to control herself?

Why had she ruined everything?

Because you're powerless over alcohol, Heather, and you

*needed God to save you, just like He's carried you through
every day of your sobriety.*

Repeating the truth gave her a feeling of calm. She had
the sudden urge to share her thoughts with Bill, but again the
words refused to come out.

Instead she stroked Choo Choo and puzzled over her father's message until they rolled up to the small airport. Checking Choo Choo in wasn't as traumatic as Heather had feared.
The dog willingly climbed into the crate. "I'll see you soon,
boy."

Choo Choo collapsed on the bottom of the crate and curled
up for a nap.

The terminal was relatively uncrowded, but still humming
with folks checking bags or waiting at their respective gates,
poking away at laptops and cell phones. She turned to thank
Bill and release him from his babysitting duties when her
eye was caught by an older person standing near a vending
machine. The woman had graying hair cut short, a cardigan
draped over one arm in spite of the summer temperatures.
She gripped a cane in the other. Something about the woman
drew Heather's attention.

A leather pocketbook hung from the lady's shoulder, worn
and scarred but somehow familiar. Very familiar. Heather
drew closer.

The woman's posture, ramrod straight in spite of her dis-
ability, struck a chord.

"Heather?" Bill said.

She ignored him and moved forward just as the woman
turned.

Heather cried out.

Her shock was mirrored on the face of the woman, who
stared openmouthed for a moment before she composed herself, gripping her cane more tightly.

"Hello, Heather."

Heather stood there, frozen in silence. Bill reached her side and took her arm.

"What is it?" he murmured, his voice low, gaze shifting from the woman to Heather. "Who is this?" he added in a whisper.

"It's…" Heather forced the words out, her mouth suddenly gone dry, her whole body trembling. "It's my mother."

Bill found himself at a loss. The two women stood there staring at each other until the older lady extended a withered hand to him.

"Margot Stark."

He shook it gently and introduced himself. "I gave Heather a ride to the airport."

Margot looked at her daughter. "Oh? Is she leaving town?"

Bill knew that this was the same woman who had walked out on Heather when she was just a child. For the life of him, he had no idea what to think about coming face-to-face with the lady now. He could tell by the emotions flooding across Heather's face that she didn't, either. Heather seemed incapable of making any kind of move, so he took her arm and led them to an unoccupied group of chairs. "I need to return a phone call. I'll be right over there."

He picked a spot where he could see them and keep an eye on the entrance at the same time. Heather didn't look at him as he moved away. Her face was dull with shock, hands gripped into tight balls on her lap.

What would this bombshell do to her? Part of him wanted to head over and tell the woman she had some nerve dropping back in on Heather's life as if she hadn't destroyed her daughter decades ago. But he thought of his own sister, Leanne, and her two daughters, grown now. No matter where Kelly and Rose went, he secretly believed his nieces would never fill the hole left by their mother's struggle with addiction and her subsequent death.

Another death he hadn't been able to prevent.

If they got the opportunity to put things right, wouldn't he want them to have it? Maybe this was Heather's chance.

Gritting his teeth, he checked his watch. The emotional drama was certainly unexpected, but it couldn't distract him from the bigger issue. The flight left in a half hour and if he had to carry Heather over his shoulder, she would be on it, mother or no mother. He tried not to listen, but their conversation carried to him anyway.

"Why are you here now?" Heather croaked.

Margot carefully laid the cane across her knees. "I had another stroke and the paralysis left me unable to manage the stairs to my apartment, much less hold down a job. To be honest, I was having a hard time meeting the rent. I called your father's cell phone. He said I could stay in the house if you would allow it."

Heather shook her head and stared. "So that's why you came back? You needed a place to live?"

"Yes. Those are the facts. You look upset. Did I say something wrong?"

Heather's mouth worked for a moment before she answered. "Wrong? What could be wrong? There's a deranged killer stalking me and now you show up." Tears began to flow down her face.

Bill tensed, waiting for Margot to reach out a hand, but her fingers gripped the cane and she did not move. He allowed himself another moment of hesitation before he found himself sitting beside Heather, an awkward arm around her shoulders. "Ms. Stark, there is a fugitive at large in Rockvale, a man named Oscar Birch who wants to punish me. He's attempting to do that by terrorizing Heather."

A flicker of fear crossed Margot's face. "I see." She nodded slowly. "So you and Heather are together, then?"

Bill flushed, grateful that Heather appeared not to hear. "No. Not anymore, but Oscar thinks so. It would be better for you not to come to this town for a while."

Margot pursed her lips, and cocked her head slightly. It was a gesture he'd seen Heather make many times. "I am an old lady now, Mr. Cloudman, and I don't have much to lose. I'll stay. But you're correct in helping Heather leave town if that is the safest choice for her."

Heather stiffened and her head came up. She stared at her mother, and the naked emotion on her face made Bill want to pull her to his chest and hide her from the world. She was overwhelmed, but underneath was an undercurrent of white-hot anger.

"I've wanted you to come back for so long," Heather said, brushing the tears from her face. "And now that you have, I'm sorry about it."

Margot blinked. "Why?"

"You should have come back to be a mother to me," she whispered. "That's the reason you should be in Rockvale, not because of your health or rent or whatever."

Margot shifted and there was a flicker of uncertainty on her face that quickly disappeared. "Heather, by now you must know I was never very good mother material."

Heather stood and cleared her throat. "That lesson I learned." She turned to Bill. "Thank you for the ride." She kissed him on the cheek and he fought every instinct to prevent himself from pulling her close.

In a moment, she was gone.

He turned back to Margot. "Ms. Stark, I still recommend you find someplace else to stay, but if you are determined to be in Rockvale, I will drive you out to the cabin."

Her eyes remained on the corridor where Heather had been a few seconds before. "Yes. That would be very good of you, Mr. Cloudman."

Bill sat uneasily behind the wheel. He'd long ago decided he would rather face an angry felon than a hysterical woman. He wished he could rewind the tape and play the whole airport scene again, only the way it should have gone. There would be a tearful greeting, Ms. Stark would beg Heather to forgive her abandonment and they'd both fly away arm in arm to put their lives back together. He wondered what Heather would be like with her mother's love in her life. Maybe if Margot had appeared earlier Heather would have escaped her battle with alcohol. Heather had told him her father had tried to be both parents to her. Bill knew that was an impossible job. He'd tried to be the parental voice of support and reason for his older sister, Leanne, in spite of the years between them.

But he hadn't come between her and the drugs.

Neither had the love of her two daughters.

He was grateful that Margot Stark appeared lost in her own thoughts until they rolled up to the cabin. He helped her from the truck and brought her bag into the house, checking thoroughly for signs of Oscar's presence. There were none, so he left her his number with instructions to call if she needed anything.

On his way out she laid a cool hand on his shoulder. "Mr. Cloudman, thank you for helping my…for helping Heather."

He nodded and continued out the door.

He did not want to be on that property anymore. There was something empty and forlorn about it now. The irony of Margot's return on the heels of Heather's departure was too much. He checked his watch. She'd be in the air soon. After a quick glance up to the cliffs that seemed to scrape the sky, he returned to the truck just as his phone rang. He smiled at the sight of the familiar number.

"Hello, Aunt Jean."

"Hey there, Billy. It's a wonder an old aunt could get such a busy young fellow on the phone."

He laughed. "I've always got time for you."

"You've always got time for my pie, more like it." Her voice grew serious. "I was remembering all those warnings you gave me about this Birch fellow and how I should be on the lookout and such."

A flash of foreboding crept up his spine. "Yes?"

"Well, I found an envelope on my porch this morning with your name on it."

Panic flashed through him. "Don't open it. Don't touch it." He was already gunning the motor to life.

"Too late. The dogs got it and I had to wrestle it away." She chuckled. "At least we know it wasn't rigged to explode."

Bill could hardly hear over his pounding heart. "Just leave it alone and I'll be there in a few minutes."

He disconnected and drove as fast as he dared toward Aunt Jean's.

SEVEN

Heather had to stop several times before she made it onto the airplane. A lacerating pain stabbed through her heart. Her mother was back, but not for her daughter. The woman had come merely for a rent-free place to live, after all the years of silence, all the years of pain. Heather had been praying since she was ten for her mother's return and now she couldn't understand why.

God, why does this have to hurt so much? And why now?

"Can I help you find your seat?" a dark-haired flight attendant offered.

Heather realized she was standing in the middle of the aisle. She shook her head and tried to take some deep breaths as she trudged to her seat.

Her mother's face was fixed in her memory and she could not tear it away.

The strong features, the perfect posture.

The hands that she had longed her whole life to hold.

Think about Miami. You can start over, away from Mother and Oscar.

And Bill.

She felt his concern in the way he'd put an arm around her shoulders.

His job was to get you on the plane, Heather. Don't mistake his actions for anything else.

So many years, she thought. So many years it had taken for her to recognize that the root of her bad decisions, her helplessness against alcohol, was the blinding need to ease the hurt from her mother's abandonment. She did not understand for one minute why her father would allow his runaway wife back in his own life. He'd never officially divorced her, and Heather didn't understand that, either. Surely Margot had hurt him as badly as she had hurt Heather by walking away without a backward glance.

Skin stinging with cold and emotion, she listened again to her father's voice mail message.

I'm asking you to take care of...

Heather filled in the rest.

Your mother.

Take care of the woman who had left her? Walked out and never looked back? His request was another slap of betrayal. She fought a surge of helplessness that she had not felt since she'd gotten sober, the nasty spiraling storm that thundered through her. Was there no one left to be her safety in this storm? Squeezing her eyes shut, she prayed a clumsy, stumbling prayer.

Help me. Please.

She willed the passengers to board the plane, to get the machine off the ground and as far away as possible. Sunlight pouring through the round window caught her attention and she peered down on the tarmac below. Some orange-vested workers bustled around, driving small carts and talking into radios.

She peered closely at their faces. Was Oscar down there somewhere? Blended in with the employees? Would he decide to go after Bill in earnest after she was gone?

Nothing will stop this guy....

Her hands began to shake and she had trouble breathing. Mother, Oscar, Bill. Her world was spiraling out of control and the only thing that would help was to leave this place immediately.

The flight attendant appeared at her side again. "Are you okay, ma'am? I notice you look upset. Are you afraid of flying?"

Yes. Afraid of flying back into the dark world she'd left. Afraid of being alone again, trapped by her own addiction.

"I'm fine, thank you. How much longer until takeoff?"

"About twenty minutes. Please let me know if I can get anything for you." She drifted away.

Heather tried her father's number again, but there was still no answer.

Twenty more minutes. She ground her teeth as time seemed to stand still.

Miami, Miami, she silently chanted. Things would be okay there. She'd find somewhere to stay, somewhere quiet, near the beach maybe. She and Choo Choo would make another life.

The realization hit her like a slap. In Miami, or South Dakota or some tropical island that was as far away as east from west, she would never escape the pain that assailed her at that moment.

Her mother's betrayal.

Her father's devotion to his wife.

Her ruined relationship with Bill.

The tatters of what had been a promising career.

There was only one escape.

Just as there had been only one way out of her alcoholism.

She had to trust Him.

And herself.

The only choice was suddenly clear in her mind as if it had

been written in fluorescent paint on the cabin wall. It was a choice that would hurt deeply, she was certain, and she was not sure she could survive it.

Lord, help me to do it. Help me to be strong.

Standing on shaky legs, she squeezed by the stream of boarding passengers. The flight attendant looked up in surprise.

"Is there something you needed?" she asked.

"I need my dog. I'm getting off this plane."

Bill pushed the truck so fast the movement rattled his teeth. On the way he phoned Crow and asked him to relay the situation to Rudley.

"Is it wired?" Crow asked breathlessly. "Should we get the bomb squad again?"

"She's already moved it. I'll be there in five more minutes and give you an update."

He disconnected as he thundered onto reservation property, ignoring the curious glance from a mechanic at the small garage. Of course Oscar would switch targets when Heather was gone. The only other person close to him, the only soul who mattered, was Aunt Jean.

She's strong, Bill. She can take care of herself.

It was true. A white woman who came to South Dakota as a twenty-year-old, doing research for a book, Aunt Jean had moved to the reservation when Bill was just a boy, shortly after his mother died. She fell in love with the place and the people and became an adopted aunt to himself, his sister and a score of other kids just as surely as if they were blood. She was strong from her endless efforts in the garden and easily commanded her pack of three dogs, leaving no room to wonder who was in charge. She was also as good a shot with a rifle as Bill. Except for the limp left by her recent fall, she was hale and hearty for her sixty-seven years.

It made him feel better to think of that as he tore off the main road down to the hollow where Aunt Jean's trailer stood in the shade of a cluster of cottonwood trees. She was in the small fenced yard, tending the pumpkins in her garden, which glistened in the intense sunlight. As he got out of the truck, her three mixed-breed dogs barked at him until Aunt Jean corrected them. They settled on whipping their tails back and forth to express their excitement.

He let himself in through the gate and wrapped his aunt in a hug, relief flooding through him. "I'm glad you're okay."

She laughed, tanned skin wrinkling into a million creases. "Why wouldn't I be okay? I've never been hurt by an envelope yet. Come in."

"Where's the envelope, Aunt Jean?"

She led him into the trailer, which was cool and filled with the smell of pickled watermelon rind. Jars of the stuff lined the counter.

"I'll find it. Sit." She handed him a glass of tea. "I saw the wanted posters the Tribal Rangers hung up. Oscar Birch the one who trashed your place?"

Bill looked at her. "How did you know about that?"

"Saw it on the *Desert Blaze* website."

He groaned. "Heather wrote it."

She smiled again. "I understand the *Blaze* wants to send someone to look at those fossils in my backyard. Seen Heather much?"

He tried to keep his tone calm. "She just flew out of town. Aunt Jean, I need to see the letter now. We can talk about Heather later."

She pursed her lips. "You can send her to the moon, Billy, but until you're honest with yourself about her she'll always be tangled around your heart."

He stood. "The envelope, Aunt Jean."

"Never were a patient one, were you? How tired you look. I pray every day that God will send you peace."

He resisted the urge to fire off a retort. God had sent him only grief by taking Leanne. And Johnny.

His heart added the other name.

And Heather.

He shook off the thought. "Are you going to give me that envelope or do I need to root around here and find it myself?"

She laughed. "You're a terrible liar. You would never poke through my trailer."

He flushed. She was right. He would not rummage through her things any more than he'd paw through a woman's purse, unless it was absolutely necessary. Even when he had to arrest female lawbreakers, he felt a flicker of unease at violating the sanctity of a woman's belongings. He held out his hand. "The envelope."

She pulled it from a cubbyhole next to the fridge. "Here you go."

He tried to take it, but she held tight, her face suddenly grave. "You are not responsible for Johnny's death. Catching Oscar won't lift that burden of guilt. Leave it for the police, Billy."

Knowing that there was probably no chance of getting any fingerprints off the envelope, before he opened it he nonetheless took it by the corner and slid on a pair of latex gloves he'd taken from the truck.

There was no message.

Only a phone number.

He looked up to find Aunt Jean watching him closely. "What does it mean?"

He sat back and tried to still the pounding in his heart.

"It means Oscar wants to talk."

* * *

Heather waved to the owner of the Rockvale Laundromat, whom she was fortunate enough to run into at the airport where he was dropping off his daughter. He'd offered her and Choo Choo a ride back to town, which she'd gratefully accepted.

As they approached the cabin, the tension knotted her stomach. Her mother was in that house. Or at least the woman who had given birth to her.

She thanked her gracious driver again and helped Choo Choo out of the car. The walk to the front door seemed endless. She wasn't certain if she should knock or unlock the door and let herself in. Who belonged there anyway? She didn't know.

The sun beat down on her with typical afternoon ferocity.

Choo Choo pushed his wet nose into her thigh to urge a decision from her, but she felt rooted to the spot. Would her mother be inside, reading quietly in the old rocking chair with the tattered cushion? Or preparing a pot of tea?

Her mother was home. A dream come true.

So why did it feel like a nightmare?

Try as she might, she could not make herself walk through the door, to see the indifferent look on her mother's face when she arrived.

She would take care of her mother to please her father.

But she didn't have to like it.

She turned back, hopped into the Jeep, Choo Choo beside her. "I've got to go see Aunt Jean about those fossils anyway, Choo. Might as well be now."

When she'd gotten off the plane, she'd resolved to face her problems instead of hiding...but there was no reason she had to face this one right away. Knowing she was taking the coward's way out and feeling a surge of guilty relief anyway, she dialed Dr. Egan's number and got his voice mail.

"Hello, Dr. Egan. I'm on my way to check out the fossil find I told you about." She gave him the address and asked him to meet her there. "I'd really appreciate your expertise." It was a long shot, but she hoped he might be interested enough to stop by or provide some quotes.

Deep down she knew from the moment she'd come face-to-face with her mother in the airport there had been no hope of a happy reunion. She felt the same about losing Bill. The only thing left was her career. Sitting up straighter, she picked up the pace.

What would she tell Bill about her return? For a fleeting moment she imagined him welcoming her, wrapping her in the kind of warm embrace he'd shared with her in better times. But those times were gone. She would stay out of his way, live carefully and not take any unnecessary risks until Oscar was caught. Remembering the intense anger in Bill's eyes as he'd handed her the photos, she knew things would come to a head quickly. There was too much rage on both sides to keep under wraps for long. Suppressing a shudder, she drove onto the reservation and headed for Aunt Jean's trailer.

As soon as she saw Bill's truck, she braked and tried to turn around, but it was too late. Bill was just exiting the trailer and he stopped midstride when he saw her. His eyes widened.

Heart beating fast, she got out and faced him.

"I'm back."

He glowered. "I see that. Why?"

"It didn't feel right running away."

He took a breath so deep it strained the front of his T-shirt. "You were supposed to get yourself to safety. You remember who is targeting you, right?"

"Of course. How could I forget it? I just…needed to come back."

There was a long pause and she felt his eyes on hers, searching for the real answer.

"It's because of your mother," he said quietly.

She squared her shoulders. "Not her, my father. He asked me to take care of her and I will respect what he wants, just until he comes back."

"Your father would want you to be safe." The anger had drained from Bill's tone, leaving an undercurrent of something softer, and the understanding there made her feel weak in the knees. She could not have sympathy now, or she'd break down. No sympathy, not from him. She did not deserve it.

"I'm here to talk to Aunt Jean about the fossils on her property."

"I don't want you near Aunt Jean. She got a note from Oscar."

Heather's mouth fell open. "Is he stalking her now, too?"

"It was a message for me." He held up a note. "A phone number. The FBI is tracing it right now."

Heather felt a chill. "He's getting daring."

"We're way beyond daring. You need to go home now. I'll talk to Rudley and see if we can make arrangements for your protection."

Aunt Jean and the dogs emerged from the trailer. The dogs barked and sniffed joyfully at the new canine arrival from behind the low fence.

"Hello, Heather. It's been a long time," Jean called over the yapping.

Heather felt herself flush. The last time she'd seen Aunt Jean, the woman had cooked a lovely meal for her and Bill, obviously thrilled at their dating. She'd given her homemade jam and invited her to return anytime.

Aunt Jean, though she'd never had children, was what

Heather imagined a mother should be. Warm and welcoming, supportive of Bill and interested in his world. After the visit Heather had felt the same swirl of despair and sought to ease the pain with a drink. One had led to two and then more as it always did, only this time she'd decided in her impaired condition to drive to the nearest store. A couple of wrong turns had brought her onto Eagle Rock reservation territory.

She'd remembered none of it until the flashing red lights in her rearview mirror had compelled her to stop, and then the pinnacle of humiliation had occurred when Bill pulled her over.

She cleared her throat.

"Hello, Aunt Jean. My editor said you found some fossils in your backyard."

Bill stepped forward. "I don't think it's a good idea to write that story now."

"It isn't a story about her—just a couple paragraphs about the find."

Jean nodded and beckoned her. "Come in for some tea and we'll talk about it."

"She can't come in right now, Aunt Jean," Bill said, taking Heather by the arm and moving her swiftly away until they were out of earshot. His hand moved from her arm to wrap around her waist and she found herself pressed close to his warm chest.

She tried to squirm away. "You're being a bully."

"Listen to me, would you?" he hissed. "This is not a game."

She willed herself to be still and ignore the way his arms circled the small of her back, the dark eyes that filled with emotion. "I'm going to stay. I have to earn a living."

He let go with one hand and slid his fingers up her arm until he cupped her chin and gently forced it up. "Heather, please..."

His face was filled with desperation and longing. She found herself unable to breathe, so she pulled away and he let her go. Insides trembling, she tried to control the spinning in her head. "I'm not here to hurt you, or make your life harder, truly I'm not. I know…I know I already did both those things and I won't let it happen again, but if I don't stay here I will be abandoning my mother and that would mean I'm the same as her." Heather was surprised that the thoughts tumbled out before she'd even realized she was thinking them, along with hot tears.

Bill drew close again and brushed the hair from her face, tracing one finger down her damp cheek. His touch was warm and gentle. "I've only known your mother for a few hours, and I know you're not your mother."

But maybe she was. She'd run after he'd arrested her, ignored him and the tenderness they'd shared. She'd run…just like her mother, coming back to South Dakota only when she'd heard Bill was gone. And before that, she'd spent years running to a bottle whenever she felt she couldn't face her problems.

A sudden paralyzing guilt hit her that made her want to turn and run again. Balling her fists and silently begging God, she lifted her face to his. "I'm not going to leave this time."

It might have been her imagination, but she saw the glimmer of a smile on his lips until his phone rang.

EIGHT

The hair on the back of Bill's neck rose as he recognized the voice on the line.

"Taking your time returning my call, Cloudman. Didn't you get the message I left with your aunt?"

Bill gripped the phone and turned away from Heather but she followed him, her face etched with concern.

"It's a matter of time before you're caught and sent back to jail, Oscar."

Oscar laughed into the phone. "Now, that's the tough lawman speaking. Only, you are not a lawman anymore, are you? You are a regular guy who lost his best friend and his strung-out sister."

"What do you know about my sister?" Bill spat the words.

"More than you think."

While Bill fought against a tide of anger, Heather touched his arm. The sensation brought his spinning rage down a notch and he took a breath. The man was baiting him, prodding at his most vulnerable parts. "Why don't you and I meet and settle this?" He ignored Heather's suddenly tightened grip. "This is between you and me, man-to-man."

"You're right about that, but it's so much fun to make you squirm. Watch the big tough guy cringe knowing I can get to his loved ones any time, any day. You deserve to twist in the wind." His tone was suddenly flat, seething with rage. "After all, you are responsible for taking away Autie and his mother."

Bill shook his head. It was like trying to reason with a stubborn child. "You killed your wife, Oscar, if that's what you mean. Remember?"

"I had no choice," Oscar shouted, the polite veneer gone. "What are you talking about?"

"And you killed my son, Autie, my boy."

Bill snapped into the phone, "Your boy killed a woman. He was a murderer just like his father. I helped bring him in and he tried to escape custody. The officers were doing their job and Autie gave them no other choice."

He heard only the sound of heavy breathing until Oscar spoke again. "You are responsible, no one else. My wife, my boy, they're gone because of you and now you are going to feel what it's like to lose."

A chill cut through Bill's body. "It's between you and me. Don't drag anyone else into this." *Especially not Heather.*

More laughter. "Now I've got you worried, don't I? You should be. I have total power over your life, Cloudman. You're a puppet and I hold the strings. I could kill you anytime." He whispered, "Maybe even right now. Maybe I've got a bead on you this very moment."

Bill pulled Heather into the circle of his arm, moving her toward the shelter of Aunt Jean's trailer. He wanted both women inside, and fast.

Oscar wasn't done. "But don't worry, Cloudman. When I kill you, it will be face-to-face. I want to look into your ugly mug and know that I've won. Be seeing you soon." The phone disconnected.

Bill pushed Heather and Aunt Jean into the trailer as he dialed the Tribal Ranger office. They patched him through to

Crow and Rudley, who were already on their way with some information on the phone number.

Bill wanted to sit with Heather and Aunt Jean, to ease the worry that shone on both their faces, but he couldn't make himself do it. The anger and helplessness flooded through him like a poison as he paced the floor.

"Tell us, Billy," Aunt Jean said.

He held up a hand. "I'll handle it. I don't want you upset."

Heather shook her head, eyes never leaving his face. "This involves all of us and we have a right to know. What did Oscar say?"

Bill tried to replay the stream of hatred in his mind. "He blames me for the death of his wife and son."

Aunt Jean frowned. "His wife? Hazel? But he killed that poor child not a half mile from here. How could that be your fault?"

"I don't know. And he implied he knows something about Leanne's death."

Heather looked questioningly at him, but he could not bring himself to tell her about Leanne.

Aunt Jean patted Heather's hand. "Leanne was a good girl, a great big sister to Bill and she tried her best to be a good mother to her twins, Kelly and Rose. She had a hard time beating her addiction."

He saw Heather's face flood with color. In that moment he hoped she might understand why he'd arrested her that night.

Aunt Jean chewed her fingernail thoughtfully. "We thought she'd done it. Clean for almost a year. Going to school and earning a little money doing some janitorial work at the lab, until she was found dead of an overdose."

Bill gritted his teeth. How he hated that word. Overdose. It made his sister sound like a common junkie, a piece of trash, not the vibrant, genuine person she had been. His big sister. And he'd lost her. "Egan should have told me she was using again."

Heather gave him a puzzled look. "Dr. Egan?"

"He was her boss. He knew she was recovering. He should have told me she was having trouble and maybe I could have intervened."

Aunt Jean raised her chin. "You know this wasn't Dr. Egan's fault. He was her employer—we were her family." She sighed. "We should have known, you and me."

He knew she was right. He didn't want to twist his sorrow into blame the way Oscar had done, but the pain rose up as fresh as it had been since Leanne's body was discovered.

Heather spoke, her voice soft. "Do you think Oscar was involved in her death somehow?"

He shook his head. "No. I think he wants to make me believe he has power, that he's responsible for every bad thing that's happened to me, because in his mind I'm the cause of every tragedy in his life."

Aunt Jean frowned. "Oh, Billy. He's a bad one. Anyone who could kill Hazel, that sweet lady."

"Did you know her well?" Heather asked.

"Well enough. She grew up here on the reservation. She… she was on her way back, they think, running from Oscar, but he caught her before she made it. Caught her and killed her."

Bill felt a sudden rush of anger that he could not control. He slammed his hand down on the table, making both women jump. "The fact is, Oscar is right. He does have the power because he knows the best way to hurt me is by hurting you two."

Heather put her hand over his, her voice soft, almost a whisper. "Then we will just have to be smarter than he is until you catch him."

He looked into her eyes and saw the same determined woman he'd known before. He wondered if she could see the fear in his eyes. His throat tightened.

Crow and Rudley pulled up and entered the trailer. Aunt Jean plied them with iced tea and potato chips.

Rudley took a videotape from his pocket. "We traced the call. You're not going to believe this."

Bill braced himself. At this point he didn't see how things could possibly be worse.

"The number Oscar called from was the pay phone, just across the street from Tribal Ranger headquarters," Rudley said.

Heather's mouth fell open.

Bill straightened. "That's monitored. There's a camera...."

Rudley held up a hand. "Yes, we've got him on camera. Here's a copy."

He popped the tape into Aunt Jean's VCR and they watched the gray image come into view. Oscar wore a baseball hat and plaid shirt. He made no effort to try to conceal his face from the camera. At the end of the call, he unfolded a large piece of paper and held it up.

They leaned forward.

Crow pointed to the screen. "It's a date, isn't it? Nine, one and the year?"

Bill nodded slowly. "Yes, September first."

"That's next week. What does it mean, Bill?" Heather said.

"It was his son Autie's birthday." Bill stared at the grainy image, the evil smile on Oscar's face. "It's the day he's going to try and kill me."

Heather tried to keep herself calm for Aunt Jean's sake. The woman looked pale despite her tanned skin. Her mouth opened, but she did not say anything. Heather fetched her a glass of water and watched as she drank it. After a few deep breaths, she seemed to recover.

"What can we do to help you, Bill?" She squeezed Heather's fingers. "I'm sure this young lady agrees with me that we're in this together."

Together? They certainly were drawn together by the actions of a crazed maniac, but being together with Bill meant possibly resurrecting the past, and that was a recipe for pain. She forced herself to nod anyway. "What should we do?"

Bill's tone was exasperated. "You *should* leave town, but we already tried that option."

The comment brought Heather back to the present. "My mother. I need to get home and check on her."

Bill nodded. "I'll go with you. Aunt Jean, why don't you come, too?"

She shook her head firmly. "No. I need to stay here. I'm tutoring some children in math later and I'm not going to cancel out on them because of some lunatic."

Heather saw the ghost of a smile on Bill's face. "I thought you were going to say something like that." He gestured to Crow and Rudley. "Can you keep watch on Aunt Jean?"

"I will," Crow said. "I'll stay awhile and check in every hour."

Heather wondered if he resented being asked to babysit. It didn't appear so.

Aunt Jean had a slightly bemused expression on her face. "I can perfectly well take care of myself, but if that makes you feel better, I'll make us a snack."

Heather followed Bill and Rudley outside. Rudley excused himself to go back to the station and continue the search.

"Keep your heads down and don't try any heroic stuff," he told Bill. "You're not wearing a badge anymore."

Bill's face darkened as he waited for her and Choo Choo to get into the Jeep. He slammed into his truck, gunned the engine and they began the trip back to her place, stopping only long enough for Bill to pick up Tank.

Heather brooded over the last few miles. Five days. In five days Oscar Birch was going to try his best to kill Bill, and he would use Bill's weaknesses to do it. Heather knew that right or wrong, Oscar counted her as one of Bill's greatest vulnerabilities.

Little did he know it was all in the past. She remembered the feel of Bill's arms around her as he'd pulled her protectively to himself. Her breath caught as she swallowed a wave of longing followed by the bitter sting of guilt. His own sister had died from her addiction. How had he felt seeing another woman he loved overcome by a need that had gotten out of control?

She fought down the flood of emotion. Maybe there was something she could dig up on Oscar that would help the police catch him. In the meantime, she had to earn a living and take care of her mother.

Her mother. It was still strange to believe her mother was back in her life.

Or was she? Maybe when the slow life in South Dakota began to wear on her she'd be gone again, just like before.

On the heels of that difficult thought, they pulled up to the cabin and she was surprised to see a Lexus parked in front that she recognized as Dr. Egan's. Another detail struck her with terror. The front door of the house was open.

She leaped from the car and Choo Choo followed, but Bill and Tank were faster.

"Stay here," he whispered, drawing a gun. He murmured something to Tank in a language she didn't know. The dog charged into the house, body rigid with excitement.

She knelt next to Choo Choo and circled his neck for comfort.

Heather felt as if she'd been dropped into a bad movie. Had

Oscar gotten to her mother? How would she feel if he had? Warring emotions fought inside her; fear, anger, resentment at the fact that she couldn't decide on any one emotion. Her mother shouldn't even be here.

Fear for Bill weighed on her, as well. The date caught on camera could have been a ruse. When the panic became too much to stand she crept into the house, Choo Choo at her side. There was a shout and loud barking. Both Heather and the dog broke into a run, charging forward, thoughts flying wildly through her head as she pictured her mother or Bill struck down at the hands of Oscar Birch.

The place was empty.

She frantically dashed from room to room, Choo Choo lumbering behind.

No sign of anyone.

The tumult came from outside, she realized, and she charged through the back door, running down the sloped path that led past the small porch to the wilder portions of the property.

Heart hammering, she saw three figures, indistinct because of the harsh sunlight that struck at her. With a surge of terror she realized one of the people was sprawled on the ground.

Bill watched Heather as she took it all in. The stricken person was her mother, propped against a rock, Tank on alert close to Dr. Egan, who stood, face pale, next to her. Bill could see the warring emotions on Heather's face as her glance shifted from her mother to Egan to Bill and back to her mother.

Bill holstered his weapon. "I told you to stay out front."

She shrugged, probably still trying to master her swarm of emotions. "Sometimes I don't do what I'm told."

Bill's lip curled and he almost laughed. "You don't say."

"What is going on?" She shot a tentative glance at her mother. "Are you hurt?"

Her mother shook her head. "I wanted to come take a look at the place again and I tripped. My cane went flying and I had some trouble getting back on my feet." Her lips were tight with frustration, or maybe it was disgust. Heather could not be sure.

Dr. Egan cleared his throat. "She heard my car pull up and called for help. I let myself in and found her."

"Fortunately, I forgot to lock the door."

Bill bit back a reprimand as Egan continued.

"We were just about to move back in the house when Bill and the attack dog came charging in." He chuckled. "Nearly scared us both out of our wits."

"Tank will do that," Bill said, giving the dog a pat.

Heather wiped at her forehead. "Let's go back into the house and we can talk." She glanced at her mother. "Are you able…?"

"Yes," Margot snapped. "Quite able, thank you." She grabbed the cane from Egan's hand and pulled herself up, ignoring his offered hand. Shoulders straight as ever, she made her way back to the house, while they followed.

Heather lagged back to stand next to Bill. "You thought it was Oscar?" she whispered.

He sighed. "I don't know what I thought."

"Why do you look like you're still angry?"

He wondered how she always seemed to know how he was feeling. "Not angry. Egan brings back bad memories, is all."

They didn't speak anymore until they got back into the relative cool of the cabin. Egan and Margot sat on the couch and accepted glasses of iced tea. Bill stood, arms folded across his chest.

"So what brought you by here, Dr. Egan?" Heather said after she put out water bowls for the two dogs.

"I got your message about the fossil find and my curiosity was piqued. That's part of the thing I love about this area. The paleontological history is stunning. The Badlands are known for their abundance of fossil mammals, but there's a good quantity of nonmammalian and plant fossils, as well." He smiled. "Sorry. I get carried away sometimes. Anyway, I called Jean's place to see if you were still there."

Bill felt a scowl form on his face at the familiar use of his aunt's name. He stared at Egan intently. "Haven't seen you at Aunt Jean's since I've been back."

Egan seemed to come to some decision. He squared his shoulders. "You made it clear that you don't want me around your aunt, Bill."

Bill stared at him. "You know why I feel that way."

"As I said before, I had only suspicions that your sister was using drugs when she worked for me. If I had had proof—seen her shooting up, let's say—I would have come to you, but families are complicated and I wasn't sure it was right to go to her brother with suspicions."

Bill's eyes flickered and he looked away momentarily. A suspicion might have been enough for him to save her life. But, situation reversed, would he have intervened if it had been Egan's sister? A man he hardly knew? He shook his head. "That's in the past."

Though he did not make eye contact, he felt the doctor's gaze on him.

"I think maybe it's not," Egan said softly. He drained the glass of tea as the phone rang.

Bill and Heather exchanged a dark look. "Let it ring," he mouthed to her. If it was Oscar, he didn't want to confirm that Heather was home. Perhaps Oscar might think that Heather had flown out of town. He didn't believe it was likely, but the guy had to make a miscalculation sometime.

An angry voice poured through the answering-machine speaker. "Fernandes, someone hacked into our site using your password. You can see the results for yourself. I'm giving you ten minutes to see before I take it down." There was muffled swearing on the answering machine. "Get me a real story by tomorrow night, and I'm not kidding around. Mr. Brown left a message for you to come see him tomorrow. Write that one up if you want, but get me something."

Heather finally made it to the phone just as the "end of message" tone sounded. "What in the world is he talking about?"

Bill gestured to her laptop, a feeling of dread in his gut. "The online site for the *Blaze*. Pull it up."

They all crowded around Heather as she booted up the computer and accessed the website. The story materialized in a moment.

No title, the font larger than the rest of the site.

Obituary for Bill Cloudman. On September 1 former Tribal Ranger Bill Cloudman will be tried, found guilty and executed for the crime of putting to death an innocent boy, Autie Birch. Cloudman has lived in shame since he allowed his partner, Johnny Moon, to walk into a deadly explosion to protect himself at the expense of a young man who trusted him. Bill lost his partner, his badge and his town by his cowardice. He will not be missed.

NINE

He heard Heather gasp as she read her own name on the byline. She looked at him, eyes round with horror. "Bill...I never..."

He squeezed her shoulder. "I know. Oscar hacked into the system. Your editor will take it down soon."

Margot's voice jerked him from his reverie. "Is this the man who is stalking you?"

Egan whistled. "If he's able to hack into your work system, who knows what else he can do?"

Heather groaned. "I'm going to lose my job."

He wanted to hold her, to apologize for jeopardizing her work, but she was up and pacing.

"I've got to get my editor a story."

"The fossils—" Egan suggested.

Bill cut him off. "No. No one is crawling around my aunt's property until this thing with Oscar is resolved."

Heather mumbled to herself. "It will have to be Mr. Brown's story. I'll write up the uranium thing tomorrow. Take some pictures. It will buy me some time."

Margot cocked her head. "Uranium? That's my field. I can help you. Take readings, if I can find the equipment."

Heather's face was awash in disbelief. A little girl's face peeked out of the woman's, tender and vulnerable. Seeing that look on her face was almost too much for him. Though he wanted to tell Heather to forget it, to stay inside and let things slide until Oscar was brought down, he would not sever the delicate thread that bound mother and daughter at that moment.

Heather was still gaping at her mother when Egan spoke up. "I can lend you the equipment. I'll bring it tomorrow."

Heather alternately went pale and then flushed pink. "Oh... okay. Tomorrow, then."

Egan walked to the door. He turned to Bill before he left. "I really did like your sister very much, Mr. Cloudman. I was trying to help her by getting her that janitorial job at the lab. I wonder every day if I made a mistake not telling you about my suspicions."

Bill nodded slightly. The thought came from the dark place inside. *Yes, you did and you won't find forgiveness here.*

Margot was fingering the top of her cane. "It's settled, then. We'll go tomorrow and see if we can get you a story. I think I'll lie down for a while now." She got up and limped down the hall.

Egan left, closing the door softly behind him.

Heather stood with a dazed expression on her face. "She offered to help. She knows it's a rag magazine, a trash paper."

He felt his heart fill. "And she knows it's important to you."

Heather's eyes brimmed and she bit her lip. "But she doesn't care. She never cared. She left me and Dad."

Before he realized it, he had her in his arms and he was caressing her back, his lips brushing across her hair, inhaling the subtle scent of her. "People do terrible things, Heather, even to the ones they love."

"This is too much," Heather cried into his chest. "I don't know what to think or feel."

He sighed, enjoying her softness. "I can't give you any advice there. I'm no good at the tender stuff."

She pulled away and looked at him, a tear glistening in each eye. "You used to be before...."

He put her gently away from him as reality once again seeped in. "Everything changed for me, Heather. Now I've only got anger left. That's a good thing, in one way."

Her face was pained. "How?"

"Because I'm going to use every ounce of that rage to bring down Oscar Birch once and for all. He's not going to hurt you or anyone else ever again." He walked to the door, missing the feel of her in his arms. "I'll be back tomorrow. Don't go anywhere until I'm with you."

He called to Tank and hastened out the door, anxious to leave before those tears left a sad trail down her cheeks.

Heather made omelets for dinner and she and her mother sat at the same banged-up wooden table they had when she was a child. They both ate little. The conversation was strained to the point of being painful.

Finally Heather said, "You don't have to help with the story."

Her mother looked at her gravely. "I know. I want to."

"Why?" Heather blurted out, the need to know overwhelming her anger. "Why? After all these years?"

Her mother put down the fork. "What you really want to know is why I left, isn't it? How I could turn my back on you?"

Heather looked at her plate, suddenly terrified to hear the next words out of her mother's mouth. She wanted to run from the table, but she was rooted to the spot.

"I am and have always been a driven person. I wanted to be a geologist like my father from the time I was a child. I never knew my mother, so I don't know how many of my traits came from her. I planned out my life, my degrees, my work at the university, and it went exactly as I envisioned until I met your father." She sighed softly. "He was doing construction on the college where I was a professor. We were totally wrong for each other, complete opposites, and I loved him instantly."

Heather nodded. Her father had said as much in the rare moments when he shared at all, but it was strange listening to her mother talking about something as intimate as their love story.

"We married with the understanding that we would never have children, because I didn't want any."

Heather winced, afraid to look her mother in the eye. "But I came along."

"Yes, and I had a stroke shortly before delivering you. I am not sure which was more overwhelming to me, the stroke or being a mother. Both seemed to me like punishments."

"Punishments?" Heather wanted to sweep the plates from the table. "I was a punishment to you? Most people love their children, think of them as blessings."

Margot held up a hand. "The only thing you have always been able to count on from me is honesty. That is how I felt. I was overwhelmed and underequipped to deal with both situations. The stroke left me unable to do my work at the university, so when you were six your father brought us here. He thought the environment, being away, would help. It didn't. I felt more isolated, further removed from myself and my goals than I ever had before."

Heather felt the tears flow, in spite of her effort to control them. "I couldn't help being born. God didn't send me here to punish you."

Margot's voice grew soft. "I know that now, but I had no idea how to be a mother. In the end, I decided that I had no business continuing in a role I was unable to fill. I was sure you'd be fine without me."

The words dropped like bombs in the quiet of the kitchen. "Fine?" She almost choked on the words. "I'm not fine. I'm a recovering alcoholic, Mother. Did you know that? No, I guess you didn't. You never bothered to check in."

"Actually, I did. Several years ago I contacted your father and asked him about you. He told me about your struggles. I asked him not to tell you I called."

Heather ignored her own surprise. "You must have been so disappointed to find out about me. I used to be a respected writer until I messed up so badly I got fired."

Margot shifted, and for a moment Heather thought she was going to touch her, but her hand remained suspended in the air. "No, your father told me how you picked yourself up and faced it, how your God helped you get through it." Her eyes flickered. "That was more than I ever had the courage to do."

A myriad of thoughts and memories swept through Heather until she found herself unable to speak at all.

Her mother got to her feet. "I don't know if I've made things better or worse between us, but I hope I have not added to your pain. Good night, Heather." She shuffled down the hall and quietly closed the bedroom door.

Heather let the emotions shudder through her until she found herself on her knees, Choo Choo licking her face.

God, show me how I'm supposed to feel.

She'd been a punishment to her mother, a crippling weight around her neck, yet there was a hint of something else in the words. Pride? A shadow of love?

You picked yourself up and faced it, her mother had said.

And she'd cared enough to keep tabs on Heather's recovery.

But not enough to come back.

That was the excruciating truth of the matter. Her mother had never felt enough for her daughter to come back.

Heather cried until there were no more tears left. Unable to sleep yet unwilling to continue brooding on her relationship with the woman in the next room, Heather wiped her eyes and sat again at her laptop. Her gaze fastened on the calendar hanging on the wall.

September first loomed just a scant five days away.

There must be something, anything she could do to help catch Oscar before he killed Bill. Fingers cold, she pulled up the *Blaze* website, relieved to find that the hideous obituary was gone and no more rants from Oscar added in its place. The passwords had been changed, security shored up, she imagined, as much as the run-down, cash-strapped newspaper could manage.

She should be researching the uranium angle. It was the most serious topic her editor had allowed her to cover. Mr. Brown believed his well was contaminated by a nearby uranium pit, but the man was known to complain about everything, from kids hanging out on his sprawling property to cars on the once-empty streets since the DUSEL had moved in. In spite of the time, she risked placing a call to him, leaving a message that she would be there the following morning. She went to pull up her notes, but a sense of urgency took her in another direction as the clock chimed ten.

It was almost Saturday. If Oscar was serious about his deadline, Bill had only four more days to live. Controlling the tremor that rolled down her spine, Heather typed Oscar's name in the search box and began to sift through the bits and pieces of his life.

There was not much to learn. Oscar, Autie and Hazel, a former Eagle Rock resident, lived in a small place outside town. Oscar kept to himself, according to the few people who came into contact with him. One report from a shop owner said he noticed bruises on Hazel Birch when she came into the store to buy groceries. Hazel's explanation was that she'd tripped and fallen.

Autie was homeschooled, apparently. He and his father would venture into town infrequently, once arriving to enter and win a shooting contest. Oscar's quote to the paper after winning was "My shooting speaks for itself."

She bit her lip. Is that how it would end for Bill? One quick shot out of nowhere? No, Oscar had made it clear in his last message. Oscar would be face-to-face with Bill at that awful moment. She remembered the coldness in Bill's eyes that belied his warm embrace.

Now I've only got anger left, he'd said.

She was a part of it. If she hadn't run, would he have been able to hang on to some tender emotions?

She pushed away the thoughts and pulled up another article describing what authorities believed had happened to Hazel. It had occurred in mid-September, and although Heather had been in Rockvale at the time, she'd been far too preoccupied with trying to hide her own addiction from Bill to remember the details.

Hazel's body was found on the Eagle Rock reservation, not far from Aunt Jean's place. She was shot with a gun later found in Oscar's possession. Her abandoned car was discovered by Al Crow in a nearby ditch with the keys in the ignition, leading police to believe that she'd been driven off the road. In a panic she'd tried to flee on foot when Oscar caught up with her. There was a picture of the abandoned car, door open, a tube of lipstick lying on the ground.

Heather tried to imagine what Hazel's frantic flight must have been like. Something made her fear for her life, so she ran, grabbing a few dollars maybe and her phone if Oscar allowed her to have one. What would it be like to leave behind any kind of safety, any means of support? Heather had done something similar when she'd fled to Miami, but she'd had the love of her father and a small amount of money to keep body and soul together.

After the murder, Oscar fled, escaping capture until he was cornered by Bill and Johnny a month later, just after Heather left town. Finally captured by the FBI, Oscar was remanded to jail, pending his trial at the federal courthouse.

But the jail hadn't held him, Heather thought. Not after his son was killed.

She glanced at the clock, now showing almost 1:00 a.m. Her eyes burned with fatigue. What had she learned that might help Bill? Nothing.

The relentless ticking of the clock followed her down the hallway as she made her way to bed.

TEN

Bill drove to Heather's before the sun came up. The house was still and dark, the land around it showing no sign of life except for the rustling of creatures in search of their last feed before the dawn.

Tank cracked a bleary eye from the passenger seat.

"I know it's early. You can nap later."

With a grumble, Tank rolled over and went to sleep.

Bill turned the situation over again in his mind. There was some way to locate Oscar and he would find it, before the man unleashed any more violence against the people in Bill's life. Heather's stark expression rose in his mind again and he remembered the feel of her in his arms. He'd felt a stirring of the old emotions, the old Bill, the one who had loved and laughed and lived. It hurt too much, reminded him of too many emotions that had begun to wither when Leanne was killed and ended when he'd let Johnny die.

He pictured Leanne, the pride on her face when she announced she'd finished her drug rehab program.

I'm going to do it this time, Billy. I'm going to show my girls that I can be a mom to them.

Then it was Johnny's voice echoing in his memory, his laughter, his enthusiastic "Morning, boss."

When the pain reached an unbearable level he muttered only one word.

"Lord…" he began. The word startled him and he clamped his mouth closed.

No.

He would not go there ever again.

The Lord had been blown out of his life by the same explosion that killed Johnny, the same tidal wave of addiction that took his big sister.

He was startled at the beep of his phone.

Crow's voice boomed across the line. "Hey. Figured you'd be up. Where are you?"

"Outside Heather's place. She's bent on working a story about that uranium pit mine. I'm keeping tabs on her."

"On old man Brown's property? He's got fangs. I'll come along in case you need backup."

Bill knew it wasn't old man Brown Crow was thinking about. "It's your day off, isn't it?"

"No days off until Oscar is brought down. Anyway, Rudley is bringing in people and making sure we Tribal Rangers have nothing to do but write parking tickets."

Bill sighed, familiar with the conflict between the Feds and local cops. He was about to ask a question when Crow answered it.

"Your aunt Jean is visiting the Tribal Council this morning to lobby for her preschool idea. She'll be in a crowd all day and we've got people looking in on her."

Bill felt a surge of relief. "Any new tips coming in from all those wanted posters?"

"Nothing. All's quiet."

"Too quiet." He disconnected, watching the first blush of sun top the massive cliffs. Where was Oscar? He had to be somewhere close, somewhere with access to the internet in order to have hacked the *Blaze* website.

Fifteen minutes later, Crow pulled up next to Bill's truck. He was dressed in jeans and a faded T-shirt. "Good thing I'm a morning person."

"Thought you'd bring your Falcon."

Crow looked away. "Loaned it out."

Bill raised an eyebrow. Crow's old Ford Falcon was a source of pride. He started to comment when the front door opened and Heather stepped onto the porch, her hair pulled back into a neat ponytail.

"Are you guys going to come in for coffee or sit there talking to the dog?" she called to Bill.

Crow grinned. "She's got your number, all right."

Bill climbed out and went into the house. Tank trotted off to give Choo Choo a thorough sniffing. Both men accepted mugs of steaming coffee and Crow walked to the far window, gazing out as he sipped.

Shadows smudged Heather's eyes, marking a poor sleep. Bill noticed some paper on the table, printouts of articles about Oscar. "I told you—"

She cut him off. "I know what you told me, but first, I'm a journalist, research is my life, and second, I'll never be able to make a living with a police detail following me, so I figured I could try to help out."

Was there a third reason? Did the strange flicker in her eyes mean she was afraid for him? He took a gulp of coffee and burned his tongue in the process. He looked around for Margot, lowering his voice. "How did things go last night?"

She flushed, leaving two high spots of color on her cheeks. "She was…honest. Having a baby, having me, was a punishment of sorts."

He did not know what to say. No words would ease the terrible sting of that revelation.

She fiddled with the pitcher of cream. "But she kept tabs on me, which I didn't know. And I think…" She shook her head suddenly, setting the ponytail bobbing. "I don't want to talk about it."

Crow rejoined them for a refill. Egan arrived at the same time Margot emerged from the bedroom, dressed and wearing a brimmed hat. She had a small pack strapped around her waist.

"Good morning, everyone," she said. "I hope I didn't keep you waiting. I must have been more tired than I realized."

Bill could see the fatigue in her lined face and wondered if she'd regretted sharing so honestly with her daughter. Heather busied herself throwing items into her own bag. "I need to talk to Mr. Brown and get his side of the story, shoot some photos of the abandoned uranium pit and his well."

Margot nodded. "I can take water and soil samples."

Egan held up a box. "Got the supplies right here. I'll have the lab run the tests, if you'd like."

Margot nodded. "Thank you. Are you sure it isn't an imposition?"

Egan sighed. "Frankly, weekends are pretty wide open for me and I can't think of anything more interesting than doing a little fieldwork."

Margot laughed. "Spoken like a true geologist."

They made arrangements to split up into two cars. Bill felt Heather's hand clutch at his arm. She didn't speak, but he read the anxiety in her face.

"Heather can come with me. Dr. Egan and Margot, you can ride with Crow," Bill said.

Heather gave him a thankful squeeze that sent tingles up his arm.

As they headed for the door, she stopped short. "In going over the old clippings, I thought of something. What about the purse?"

Bill nearly plowed into her. "What?"

"Hazel's."

Crow stepped closer, forehead creased. "Hazel Birch? Oscar's wife?"

"Yes. If she was planning to leave town, she'd have brought her purse. I thought of it when I saw the picture of the abandoned car. There was a lipstick there on the ground. Most women carry that kind of thing in a purse." She turned to Crow. "Was there a purse with the body?"

"No, no purse. Nothing like that."

"That's strange," Heather said.

Crow's face darkened. "Are you saying I didn't do my job? That I missed finding a purse? You don't think some dumb Indian can do sophisticated police work?"

Bill put his hand up. "Hey. She didn't say anything like that. She's asking a question, that's all."

Crow's gaze shifted from Heather to Bill and back again. "Yeah, okay. Sorry. I guess I'm feeling the heat, with the Feds calling all the shots around here." He shrugged apologetically and headed for the car.

Heather's eyes were round with surprise. "I didn't mean to suggest he wasn't doing his job."

"I know. He's just wound up. We're all wound up, which is why I still think—"

"I'm going to get my story. Don't even try to talk me out of it." She bent to pat the dog. "You stay here, Choo. Mama will be back soon." Shouldering her purse, she walked out.

With a deep sigh, Bill followed her.

The drive to the old uranium mine took them over ten miles of twisted, dusty road that climbed gently until they reached a wide prairie studded with stretches of scrubby grass and odd-shaped clusters of bleached rock. As they traveled upward past the gullied ridges and eroded hills, Heather was reminded of a moonscape. Here and there were some wild buckwheat, clinging in wiry tufts to the rock, growing ever sparser until they arrived at the pit, a sprawling crater that shone silver in the morning sunlight.

Margot shaded her eyes with her good hand as she peered in. She pointed to the west. "If I've figured it right, this pit lies above the far edge of Charlie Moon's property, doesn't it?"

Heather frowned. "True."

"Has Charlie ever voiced a concern about his water quality?"

Dr. Egan started. "As a matter of fact, he hasn't, but the water was tested anyway. I don't know why I didn't remember it. Shortly after I came here, the lab was making plans to buy a parcel of land to build some employee housing. Charlie was interested in having his property considered, so a team of USGS guys went to do some sampling and map the area. I was asked to consult."

Bill gestured for him to continue. "So what was the outcome?"

"No problems, I think, but the economic situation changed the plan. The lab postponed buying any more land."

Bill sighed. "So Charlie's got no way out."

Heather felt like taking his hand. She knew he felt a terrible burden of responsibility for Charlie and Tina Moon. A lucrative offer on their land would have at least ensured a future for the little girl. She knew Bill felt powerless about the situation.

Unable to think of anything helpful to say, Heather got to work. She took some pictures of the gaping hole, which had been abandoned, according to her research, when the supply of mined uranium began to exceed the demand in the mid-1960s. Many mine owners had simply walked away, leaving the question about radioactive contamination unanswered.

Heather noticed her mother scraping some soil samples into test tubes and almost smiled. Thorough. She hardly knew anything about her mother, but she had already learned the woman was meticulous. She had vague memories from Miami when the Fernandes family would collect shells at the beach and her mother would help her carefully organize them into neatly labeled collections. If only life were so easily put into an orderly arrangement.

Margot shaded her eyes and glanced out along the sprawling acres and the rising cliffs beyond. "There are caves here, I'd imagine," she said, a dreamy look on her face. "Reminds me of my undergraduate work."

Dr. Egan laughed. "Mine, too. I spent months helping at an excavation site of a sinkhole. The professor in charge was certain it was the perfect spot to find mammoth fossils."

Margot's eyes widened. "And?"

Crow snorted. "I'll bet he found nothing better than some rusty hubcaps."

Margot shot him a look. "The desert is rich in paleontological history."

He sighed deeply. "This town is rich in nothing."

Margot and Dr. Egan exchanged quizzical glances as Crow walked away.

"What did you find at the excavation site, Dr. Egan?" Margot asked.

"Some fossils of short-faced bears and some nicely preserved wolf bones, but nothing more exciting than that. He's wrong, though," Egan said, pointing at Crow's back. "The research we're doing at the DUSEL, it's priceless. It's so deep there you get no interference from cosmic rays. We're already conducting some experiments in geology and hydrology at forty-eight hundred feet."

"Dr. Egan," Heather began, eager to build a conversational bridge with the man she needed in order to resurrect her career. "I'd love to—"

"Later," Bill said, in spite of the annoyed look she shot him.

Bill hustled them back to the truck and they drove the half hour to Mr. Brown's property, crossing a sturdy bridge that spanned a river gorge gouged deep into the red earth. The water, some fifty feet below, was reduced to a sliver snaking below them as they rolled across the wooden structure.

When they got out of the cars, Heather asked the question that had been burning in her mind. "Dr. Egan, was Mr. Brown's land included in the USGS testing? His groundwater comes from the same aquifer, doesn't it?"

Dr. Egan wiped his brow and laughed. "Yes, it does, but Mr. Brown has proven to be somewhat unreliable. He's a bit of a conspiracy theorist and he decided the team was part of some plot to pour poison in his well to shut him up. I heard he chased them off the property with a shotgun."

Great, Heather thought. Her chance at a real story was going to be touted as the babblings of a lunatic. No wonder her editor had been so eager to assign it to her.

Mr. Brown did not answer her repeated knocks. Heather left a note under his doormat with her cell number. They found the well, and Dr. Egan and Heather's mother drew samples, sealing the water into stoppered bottles.

Dr. Egan went to the car to get a kit for taking soil samples.

Margot frowned. "You said Mr. Brown is afraid the uranium pit mine has polluted his well?"

Heather hesitantly drew near. "Yes. I did a little research and it's plausible. There was a lot of in situ leach mining around."

Margot nodded. "Meaning water was pumped into the ground to pull up uranium. After it's extracted, the water is eventually injected back into the aquifers. Unfortunately, when these pit mines are abandoned without proper care, the runoff can seep into rivers before it's cleaned up."

Heather noticed Bill was not interested in the sampling

or conversation. His eyes were focused on the tree line, the nearby rock pile, anywhere he thought Oscar Birch might be hiding. Crow had disappeared for the moment and Heather suspected he was checking the property, as well.

Margot looked up from her work and Heather was caught at the change on her face. She looked years younger, her eyes infused with light. A lump formed in Heather's throat at the eagerness she saw there. If only her mother felt that way about her.

"Why are you staring at me like that?" Margot asked.

Heather blushed. "Oh, you just look different. Happier."

Margot smiled. "I haven't had a purpose for a very long time, since I had to quit my clerical job at the university. It was all I could manage, but it filled the hours. It feels wonderful to be doing something again, something worthwhile."

There was a shimmer in her mother's eyes that made Heather wonder if she was speaking about something other than work. It was a ridiculous thought and Heather put it out of her head.

Bill shot them a look. "If you're done here, let's get moving. The less time we spend out in the open, the better."

Tank, who had begun to pace in small circles, let out a whine. The hair on the scruff of his neck stood up. Bill pushed Heather toward the truck. "We're leaving now."

Heather stumbled, fear strong in her stomach. Dr. Egan helped Margot quickly gather up her supplies and held her elbow as she made her way to Crow's vehicle. Heather risked a look around as Bill opened the door and propelled her inside. No sign of anything amiss that she could detect, but Tank was barking now, body taut.

"Stay here," Bill directed as he closed the door. He dialed his cell phone and waited before he snapped it shut. "Crow's not answering. I'm going to find him." He handed her the keys. "Start the engine and if there's any trouble, drive out of here as fast as you can."

Before she could answer, he jogged to the other car and gave them the same instructions. Dr. Egan sat in the driver's seat, face pale, hands clutching the steering wheel. Crouching low, Bill spoke to Tank and they both headed around the back of the house.

Tiny beads of sweat prickled Heather's forehead, in spite of the ice-cold sensation in the pit of her stomach. Oscar was waiting, hiding behind some rock or tree. She'd allowed the whole thing to happen because of her need to get the story, to humor Dr. Egan.

She swallowed.

To be something in the eyes of her mother. They should be safe at home, but once again her bad choices overrode good sense.

Teeth clenched, she pounded the steering wheel.

Why should she put all of them at risk to impress her runaway mother? A swell of anger rushed up inside her so strongly it took her breath away. Before the sensation became strong enough to overwhelm her, she closed her eyes.

"Lord, help me be strong against the hurt," she murmured. She would not give in to the darkness and let go of her hard-earned wisdom, the blessing of a sober life. When she opened her eyes, she saw Bill running to the truck, phone to his ear, Tank's barking now audible from behind the house.

ELEVEN

"Go back to town," Bill said, keeping his voice low. "Something's wrong. Saw through the window there's a bottle of whiskey on the kitchen table." He saw her raised eyebrow. "Brown doesn't drink. His wife was killed by a drunk driver and he doesn't touch a drop."

Heather blinked, then called past Bill to her mother. "Go back, Dr. Egan. I'm going to stay."

Bill reached through the window and gripped her wrist. "No, you're not. Get out of here right now."

"I can help."

"No, you can't."

She covered his fingers where his hand touched her forearm. "Bill, I...I ran away last time. I left you. I'm not going to do it again."

A surge of pain and pleasure rippled through him. Those eyes, those amazing eyes still held the embers of love he'd seen in them a year before, but now it was pure and unpolluted by alcohol. There was still love there, or the potential for it anyway, and he'd only have to reach out for it. Being so close to that possibility made him dizzy.

At the same time, the evil was mounting with every minute. The trap that he knew Oscar was setting for him would catch her, too, as it had caught Johnny. He could not watch her be destroyed. He could not watch her life snuffed out and stand by her grave to say the final goodbye. He withdrew his hand and stripped all the emotion from his face.

"Heather, the one thing you will accomplish by staying is make it harder for me to catch Oscar. That's the only thing I want, the only thing that's left for me. I want you to drive back to Rockvale and keep going."

The true meaning of what he'd said crept over her face, along with a flush. She kept her eyes on his for a moment, and then her gaze dropped to her lap.

He forced himself to wait, to breathe, to stop up the words that wanted to flood out and ease the pain on her face. He waited in silence.

She looked up, a sheen of moisture in her eyes, her chin high and strong. "I understand." She turned the key and pulled out of the long drive. Bill nodded to Egan, who followed a few yards behind.

Ignoring the tearing sensation in his chest, he turned back to the house. No response to the second call to Crow's phone. The back door of the house was secure, so where was Crow? Searching the shed? Checking the dense thicket of shrubs and dry grass that edged this part of the property?

Gun drawn, Bill was headed for the shed when the sound of movement stopped him. Tank tensed, ears pricked.

He cautioned the dog to stay. With a quiet whine, Tank obeyed until booted feet edged around the corner. Tank went wild and charged, Bill behind him shouting orders, until he realized the figure was Crow, one hand clutching his gun, the other over his heart.

"Off, Tank, you crazy dog. You scared the life out of me," Crow gasped.

Bill lowered his weapon, his face suddenly bathed in sweat. "Why didn't you answer your phone?"

"Had it on silent." Crow shook his head. "It's a pity. I found Mr. Brown."

Bill followed Crow into the shed. Mr. Brown's body was folded into a crate and he appeared to have been dead for several days. Bill had seen many bodies in his years on duty, but the sight never failed to remind him how primitive man could be. To end a life, to snuff out all that possibility in a moment of rage or selfishness. He sighed and turned away.

Bill and Crow exited the shed while Bill called the police for the second time and updated them. His eyes searched the distance, noting with relief that his truck was almost across the bridge, Egan's vehicle following.

Crow followed his glance. "Sent 'em back?"

Bill nodded. "I told Heather she and her mother should leave this town."

Crow folded his arms with a sigh. "It's the right thing."

"I know." He wondered when the raw feeling in his chest would go away. He cleared his throat. "Oscar must have been holing up here. He no doubt sent the note to the *Desert Blaze* arranging the meeting to get her here."

He stared at Crow, who reflected his unease back at him.

Crow gave voice to the thoughts. "Then where is he now? No sign of anyone. Tank's not picking up on anything."

"Maybe we arrived too early." Bill scanned the tree line, the cliffs above them, the rusty gorge, which the cars were now crossing. The timbers glimmered in the sunlight, pale against the endless sky.

His heart pounded to a stop. "The bridge…" he started, ripping out his cell phone. "Heather, get off that bridge," he shouted when she picked up.

"What?" Her voice was high, tense.

"I think he's wired the bridge. You've got to—"

An explosion ripped through the air. As he and Crow ran, he could see nothing but a mushrooming cloud of dust that obscured the view. Falling debris rained down on them, bits of wood and gravel plunging to the ground all around.

Fear thickened Bill's throat and he didn't feel the sting of falling rock. The haze of red-and-gold dirt cleared slightly as they pounded toward the gorge, feet slipping on the grit-coated ground.

He slowed as they approached the bridge, fears becoming tangible images in his mind.

A gaping hole.

The cars crushed and unrecognizable.

Heather's body broken and lifeless.

Like Johnny.

Like Leanne.

The fear seemed to pull at his legs, slowing him, fighting him like the grip of some inescapable nightmare.

As he reached the edge of the gorge, the sight struck him like a fist.

The center of the bridge was gone, a gaping and blackened wound. Gone, too, were both cars.

Heather's body was rocked by the explosion. Only her frantic stomp on the gas pedal had propelled the truck forward in time to clear the bridge before it exploded. Bill's truck shimmied and bucked from the blast, sliding into the tall grass on the narrow shoulder of the road. She sat for a moment, gripping the wheel, unable to move.

Mother.

The thought galvanized her into action. She slammed open the truck door and scrambled out.

Dr. Egan had just been starting across the bridge when she'd cleared it. Had he been able to back up? Pushing through the tall grass, she made it back to the road, the dust still rolling through the air in undulating waves.

She coughed at the choking debris, and was trying to

cover her mouth against the dirt when a hand reached out and grabbed her, twisting her arm behind her back.

She found herself slammed up against the rock wall, a soft voice hissing in her ear. "You should have flown home, girl."

Oscar turned her around roughly, took her phone out of her pocket, then let her go, stepping back quickly as though she was some sort of odious insect.

Heather fought for speech, but the terror racing through her body left her dumb.

He cocked his bald head and folded his arms. "I didn't think you would make it."

She forced the words out through the terror that paralyzed her. "I'm tough."

He blinked. "Yes, I believe you are." He turned his head to look out over the canyon. "The lady in the other car with Egan. Who is she?"

Heather didn't answer, so Oscar stepped closer. "You will answer when I speak to you," he said, taking her face in his hands, his fingers digging into her cheeks.

She tried to yank away, pulling at his arms, but his grip was too tight. For a moment she was forced to stare into his eyes and the madness she saw there horrified her. He stepped away suddenly and released her before she could kick out at him.

"Never mind," he said. "You would probably lie anyway." Her phone rang and Oscar looked at the screen. "Why, I believe it is your boyfriend. Shall I tell him you are occupied?" He dropped the phone to the ground and smashed it underneath his heel with such force that bits of plastic and metal shot through the air.

Heather's mind whirled. She could not get past him to run up the road. He would catch her, she had no doubt. The only other escape was back toward the ruined bridge in the hope that Bill was there, that she could shout for help. She eased a step away from Oscar, who seemed lost in thought.

When he looked at her again, he appeared to be weighing something in his mind. "Tell Bill I'll see him soon. We have an appointment that I intend to keep."

On the day he killed Bill.

The smug look on Oscar's face, the absolute certainty in his tone awakened a fury in her. "You are crazy. Why don't you be a man and take responsibility for what you did?"

He blinked. "For what I did? All of it, my wife, the woman, this…" He waved a hand vaguely at the bridge. "It's all because of Cloudman." The expression on his face was incredulous, as if he couldn't understand how she could be so dense.

"All Bill did was try to arrest you and your son for murdering people."

Oscar's face darkened and he strode forward, hand raised.

She drew back, scrabbling behind her for a rock or branch that she could use to defend herself.

There was a shout from the other side of the gorge. The sound made Oscar pause, eyes narrowed. "Tell him, or maybe I'll tell him myself right now," he said, and then he strode away from the gorge, following the road until he was out of sight.

Heather took off in the other direction, running, falling, stumbling over the rough ground. The shouting was louder now until she reached the edge. Forcing herself to look across the bridge, she saw Crow's vehicle dangling over the precipice. The bottom dropped out of her stomach until she saw the figures outlined in tight shadow on the other side. Her mother stood next to Dr. Egan, a few feet away from the car. They hadn't gone over the side. They were alive.

Her legs started to shake. "Thank You, God," she murmured, wondering where the deep flood of emotion sprang from. She heard the sound of an engine behind her.

Oscar? She looked across the span of wooden planks, at the burned-out hole in the middle, a narrow margin of wood intact on either side, barely holding the structure in place.

Bill stepped to the edge, shouting something she couldn't hear.

All she could feel was the terror of Oscar's fingers on her face, the cold detachment in his eyes as he justified the people he had killed. She looked again at the broken bridge, and back at the bend in the road where she knew Oscar would emerge at any moment.

A worse thought occurred to her. Oscar might be driving along the far side of the property, coming up from behind to slaughter Bill, Dr. Egan and her mother. She could try to catch him, but she knew there was no way she could over-power Oscar Birch. The fastest way to warn them was right in front of her.

After a deep breath, she stepped out onto the planks.

She heard Bill's voice clearly now.

"No, Heather," he shouted. "Go back."

She looked at her feet, carefully placing one after the other as she eased out onto the bridge.

Bill roared, "Stop!"

She ignored him. She would get back to her mother, to Bill and Dr. Egan, and Oscar would not win. He could not win.

Creeping toward the blackened beams, Heather heard the wood creaking and groaning under her weight. She kept as close to the unscorched outer edge as possible. She could hear the tense words from the other side.

"Don't," Dr. Egan said, calling to Bill. "Your weight will add too much stress."

Out of the corner of her eye she could see Bill pacing back and forth, his body tense as wire.

She blocked it all out and inched along. "Help me get across, Lord," she whispered as she moved along. Without warning a board broke, her foot plunging through. She screamed, clinging to the nearest beam to keep from falling, realizing with horror that her foot was imprisoned in the gap. Afraid to yank too hard, she tried to wriggle her ankle back and forth, but the wood refused to release her.

She eased down onto the planks and pulled, with no result. Her head throbbed as she tried to decide what to do. A vibration rippled through the wood. She jerked her head up, looking for Oscar.

It was Bill, easing along as if he was walking on eggshells.

She could not read the expression on his face. Behind him on the far side, her mother pressed a hand to her mouth. Dr. Egan leaned forward. Crow talked rapidly into his phone. All of them stared at the two on the bridge, eyes riveted to Bill's slow progress.

Bill's dark eyes found hers, glittering like obsidian as he came closer. She wanted to call out to him, to tell him to get her mother and the others away to safety, but she could only stare at him, willing him to come closer, to reach out to her.

A slight breeze pulled at her hair.

The sun beat down mercilessly.

He was close enough now that she could see the dark flash of his eyes, his clenched jaw.

Help me, Bill.

Finally his hand grabbed hers.

"I'm going to loosen your foot."

"Oscar…" she panted.

"Police are on their way." He eased closer to where her foot was imprisoned and the boards crackled ominously. He froze, sweat running down his forehead.

Her whole body trembled as he pulled away some of the splintered wood.

"Try now," he said.

She pulled her leg free, sending bits of wood tumbling into the chasm below.

"Follow me," he said, turning and crawling a few paces before gingerly getting to his feet.

It was a torturous journey.

They edged along, Bill's strong hand steadying her trembling one.

The bridge shuddered and crackled under them, bits of wood splintering to fall away as they passed.

After an eternity, they made it to the edge and stepped off. Heather's legs gave out and Bill lowered her to the ground, his arms around her, squeezing her breathless against his chest. She felt his heartbeat hammering against her face, the warmth of his tight embrace.

He pressed his face against her hair. "Heather…" His voice was ragged.

She didn't want to move, to rise. All she desired was to stay there safe in Bill's arms, the warmth of him wrapping around her like the kiss of sunshine.

Her mother came close, Crow and Dr. Egan following.

"Why would you do something like that?" Margot's stunned voice came from far away.

Oscar, she wanted to scream.

He's mad.

He won't stop until Bill is dead.

A wave of horror consumed her. She could only press herself deeper into Bill's embrace as if it were the only thing in the world that was real.

From a distance came the wail of sirens.

TWELVE

Sunday morning Bill woke to the sound of his phone. He sat bolt upright, startling Tank.

"Sorry to call so early," Heather said.

"No problem. Did you get the new phone I gave you up and running?"

"Yes, thank you." She hesitated.

He understood her awkward formality. Since they'd made it off the bridge, a strange blanket of emotion had wrapped around both of them. For his part, he could not stop thinking about her there, suspended over the gorge, face stark with terror, nor could he seem to let go of the feeling of her next to him, pressed against his chest as if she'd never left. But it couldn't be. He did not want to rekindle what they'd had. "Everything okay?"

"Yes, there's been an officer in front of the house all night."

"You and your mother comfortable?"

"I'm just scraped up a little. Mom is still asleep."

"That's good." He tried to think of what to say next.

"I remembered something Oscar said that struck me oddly."

Bill straightened. "Go on."

"He said you were responsible for the people he'd killed. I think he said 'my wife, the woman.'"

"The woman?"

"Yes. I thought it was strange, but I was too scared to ask him to clarify."

The thought of her face-to-face with Oscar made his skin crawl. "Thanks for letting me know."

"Okay." A silence filled the line. He should say something, do something. The overwhelming urge to let go of his senses and run back into her life tore at him, but he could only hold the phone to his ear until she mumbled a goodbye and hung up.

He listened for a moment to the dial tone and knew that he would not reunite with Heather Fernandes because, the ugly truth of it was, he was a coward. He could not face losing her or anyone else again. Besides, it would take all his strength and emotional stamina to go head-to-head with Oscar. So far, he was one step behind the man at every turn.

Bill flopped back down on the bed and tried to clear his mind. What woman was Oscar referring to in his last encounter with Heather? He had not been linked to any other deaths that Bill was aware of. He grabbed his phone and sent a text to Rudley and Crow. Maybe they had encountered an unsolved murder in the months he'd been gone.

Where are you, Oscar? The pay phone at the Tribal Ranger office. Mr. Brown's place. The dilapidated trailer. Oscar would be close, but not too close. Rockvale was a small town and the police had gotten the word out about the escaped fugitive, so he'd have to keep his distance or disguise himself. They'd already checked all the hotels and apartments in the surrounding areas, so it must be something else, a house or a campground, even, but it was close by, he was sure of it.

The thought dawned on him before he'd finished dressing. There was a place, the perfect place where Oscar could get a bead on the town and still be far enough away to avoid detection. Bill threw on the rest of his clothes and headed for the truck, calling Crow on his way. There was no answer, so he left a message. He considered calling Rudley, but he knew the Feds would cut him out of the capture, and Bill was sure Oscar would do his best to kill Rudley or any other officer who attempted to bring him down.

He made it to Charlie Moon's property in record time. Charlie answered the door. "Whaddya want?"

Bill made sure Tina was not standing behind her uncle listening. "I think Oscar may be hiding out on your property."

Charlie blinked. "Here? I would have seen him." He started to close the door, but Bill stopped it.

"The caves. The limestone caves on the edge of the bluff, near Brown's property. He could be there and you would never know. He could come and go on the northern trail and you wouldn't see him."

Charlie shook his head. "I would know."

"Okay, let me go look. Just to be sure."

Charlie's face hardened. "I don't want you on this property."

Bill bit back a sharp retort. He tried for calm. "Just a quick check, that's all."

"No."

"If it will help, I'll get Crow to do it, or the Feds. I don't have to be involved."

Charlie glared. "I said no."

Bill exploded. "I can't believe you would turn a blind eye to a murderer on your property, especially the guy who killed Johnny." It was the wrong thing to say. He knew it the moment it left his mouth.

"Get out of here, Bill. From what I hear, Oscar came back to this town to get you and no one else. Frankly, the sooner he gets his business finished, the better."

The door slammed in Bill's face.

He felt like smashing his fist against the wood. Charlie Moon would risk his own safety and Tina's because of his hatred of Bill. He looked up at the cliffs that rippled along the edge of Charlie's land. The caves were clearly on Moon property, but if he climbed to the highest point on Heather's land he might be able to get a glimpse of movement, maybe catch sight of Oscar's vehicle if the man got careless.

If that happened, there was nothing going to stop him from taking Oscar down, not Charlie, not the Feds, nobody. Gun fastened to his hip and a pair of binoculars on the seat next to him, Bill headed off to Heather's.

The thought of seeing her again lit a fire inside him.

Remember, he told himself.

Deal with Oscar and give her back her life.

And keep her out of yours.

A parade of Tribal Rangers and people Heather didn't know came and went, driving on and off the property, keeping watch. She found herself looking for Bill, but she didn't see him. Hours later as the late afternoon came, there was still no sign of him. What would she do if she did encounter Bill? Her own body betrayed her at the bridge. He had no doubt felt her longing clearly in her desperate embrace.

She yearned with every pore to find him. And then what? To commit herself to Bill when he clearly didn't want her? There might be a lingering sense of affection, or maybe even a remnant of love in his heart, but he would not open himself up to her again, and she didn't blame him. For him, duty was all that was left.

His duty to find Oscar.

And then what? Heather wondered if he would find love again someday when the anger and hurt had eased. Or would he hold on to those bitter dregs without any hope in his heart?

She closed her eyes and prayed for not just his safety, but his soul.

Steering her mind to the practical, she made herself sit at the computer and type up a brief statement about the discovery of Mr. Brown's body for her editor. It pained her to reduce the man's death to a pitiful handful of words, but she had to keep that paycheck coming in. For some reason, the intense drive to resurrect her career seemed to be fading away the closer they came to Oscar's deadline. She found she no longer cared as much about the big lab story and courting a connection with Dr. Egan.

What was happening to her? To her goals and emotions?

She laid her head on her arms and closed her eyes. When she opened them, she found her mother in the kitchen, laying out an assortment of utensils. Margot had kept to herself for most of the day, emerging only to ask one of the police officers to do an errand for her.

Heather got to her feet and began to pace. "Is Dr. Egan okay? He looked pretty shaken up."

"Yes. He even managed to secure the soil and water samples and get them to his lab for testing."

"A true geologist."

"Exactly." She took eggs from the fridge and cracked them into a bowl. "I'm not much of a cook, but I can scramble us some eggs for dinner."

Heather started in surprise. Was is dinnertime already? The hours had begun to fly by with frightening speed. Sunday was coming to a close and Oscar's deadline would arrive on Tuesday.

Margot looked up from her cooking. "What are you thinking about?"

She blinked at her mother, grabbing some silverware and

napkins to keep her hands busy. She thought about making something up, but the truth came out anyway. "About Oscar. He said Bill would die on Tuesday."

Margot poured the eggs into a pan and stirred them carefully. "Bill is a good man, from what I've seen." She swirled the spatula. "Do you love him?"

The question startled Heather so much, she dropped the fork she was setting on the table. "Love him?" Her cheeks flushed. "We…we had a relationship and I ruined it with my drinking. I ran away."

"Doesn't seem like you burned the bridge completely, if you'll excuse the metaphor. He is very concerned about you."

"It's the cop in him."

"I don't think that's all of it. There's something else there."

"His sister died of addiction. He doesn't want to be with an alcoholic, recovering or otherwise."

Margot slid two plates onto the table and they sat. "Has he told you that?"

"Not exactly."

"Then you are creating a theory based on insufficient evidence."

"Hold on," Heather said, sudden anger rising along with the blood in her cheeks. "You have no right, no business telling me about relationships. You ran away, from me and from Dad."

She nodded. "Those are the facts, yes."

"Then how can you sit there and tell me Bill loves me? You don't know anything about love."

She held up two fingers. "Not entirely true. Yes, I have ruined my relationship with you and your father, but there are two facts you have not accounted for. First, your father still loves me."

Heather gaped. The sheer nerve of the woman to believe it. "You don't know that."

"Yes, I do. I'm not saying I deserve it or that I earned it, because I didn't, but the fact of the matter is he does still love me and I never really stopped loving him."

She had no right, no right at all to claim her husband's love after what she'd done. Heather felt a desperate need to change the subject before she blew up. "Believe it if you want. What's the second fact?"

Margot stopped, sipped a glass of water and crimped the edges of her napkin. "It came to me when I saw you crawling across that bridge."

"What did?"

"I've never really put much stock in God, Heather. I have always believed He was a myth created to help people feel better about their circumstances, a salve for the weak-minded."

Heather held her tongue, waiting for her mother to say what she needed to say.

"But on that bridge, I had a strange thought. Standing there, watching you make your way along, knowing you might fall at any moment, I thought that if there was a God, how very hard it must be to watch His children make their way in the world, loving them so much, yet allowing them to go through perils to find their way to Him."

The kitchen grew quiet, the ticking of the clock the only sound. Heather sat in dumbfounded silence.

"And I realized that…" Margot swallowed hard and cleared her throat. "I realized that I wanted more than anything in the world for you to cross that bridge safely for one very simple reason."

"Why?" Heather whispered.

"Because I love you."

The words were soft, like a gentle rain, but they swept

through Heather with the force of a tsunami. "You can't love me. You ran from me because I ruined your life. I'm a punishment, the reason you lost everything that was important to you."

"Precisely proving my second point. I do love you, which is as much a surprise to me as you. There's no rational reason why someone is compelled to love a person just because that being came out of their body, yet it is true. I love you, though I haven't earned the right and you will likely never return that love."

Heather forced the words out. "How is that possible?"

Margot gave her a lopsided grin. "I'm not sure. You are more the expert in these matters than I, but I think that you would probably say it's because of God, wouldn't you?"

There was no way to make sense of the mad rush of emotion that shook Heather. Her mother's words had shocked her more than anything in her entire life. Her chest squeezed tight and she shot up from her chair. For a long moment her eyes were riveted on her mother's face, then she walked to the back door mumbling something about getting some air.

It was evening, the almost full moon painting everything silver. Choo Choo followed her outside and they sat together on the step.

Because I love you.

How she'd longed to hear it, obsessed about those words.

Because I love you.

But it wasn't the way it should be, coming from a distant mother who'd let her down so hard her heart was cracked forever. Tears streamed down her face and Choo Choo pressed his chin on her lap. She hardly heard the sound of the truck until it had almost rumbled by along the dirt trail.

Bill stopped when he saw her there. She didn't think, only went to him and got into the truck, Choo Choo settling into her lap after a brief greeting to Tank in the back.

He didn't say anything but sat scrutinizing her face in the moonlight. Then he began to drive slowly along the trail and she knew he was giving her the time to pull herself together before they spoke.

She wondered as she watched him drive, his face impassive as always, how he kept his real feelings tucked inside, buried deep down like the sparkling crystals inside a rough geode. She tried several deep breaths before she spoke. "Out for a drive?"

He nodded. "Spent a couple hours spying on Charlie Moon's property. Thought Oscar might be there."

"Can the police search?"

Bill grimaced. "Charlie won't allow it and the Feds don't think there's enough evidence to procure a search warrant." He looked suddenly tired. "Might be clutching at straws anyway."

Heather watched a bat dart gracefully through the sky. "My mother loves me," she blurted out.

He stayed silent for a moment. "And that's what you've always wanted to hear."

"Yes, so why don't I feel elated? Fulfilled? Why does it make an ache so deep inside that I think I'm losing my mind?"

He stopped the truck and parked before he turned to face her, taking her hand. "I'm sorry it wasn't what you wanted it to be."

There was something else, something he wanted to say.

"What is it?" she asked.

He pulled away. "Nothing."

"Bill, I know it's not fair but there's only one person I can think of to talk to right now and it's you. Please…" Her voice broke. "Please don't shut me out."

He sucked in a breath. "I was just thinking about my sister. Our mom died when we were kids, and Dad was a drunk.

Leanne started using at age twelve and her addiction owned her by the time she was an adult. I think…I always thought that her using was a way of filling up that empty spot."

Heather felt a lance of pain. "It must have hurt you badly when you found out about my drinking."

"I wanted to save you."

"Because you remembered what happened to Leanne."

"No." His voice dropped to a near whisper. "Because I loved you."

The ache inside her grew enormous, swallowing her up in darkness. *Loved you.*

There it was, warmth and tenderness, passion and emotion, all presented to her in the person of Bill Cloudman, and she'd thrown it all away. Turned on her heel and left him behind, just as her mother had done.

On impulse she reached over and cupped his face in her hands, feeling the strength there, stroking his cheeks, suddenly moving her lips to the sharp angles of his cheekbones, the curve of his chin, inhaling the warmth of him. His fingers tensed on her shoulders as he pulled her closer for a moment. She could hear the faintest sigh before he gently moved her away from him.

He didn't speak, only shook his head slightly, and the gesture told her everything.

The hard truth mocked her. She loved Bill Cloudman intensely, just as if she'd never left.

Her mother's words could just as easily be her own.

I love you, though I haven't earned the right and you will likely never return that love.

She loved Bill and he could not love her back.

Not again.

Bill suddenly straightened. She tried to still her thundering heart as a vehicle rolled down slowly from the upper trail, headlights dark.

She could not make out the type of vehicle or the driver, but she did not have to.

Bill was already out of the car and running.

THIRTEEN

It didn't make sense. The vehicle was big, rolling along slowly as if the driver was trying to look out the side window as he moved. Bill ran, head down, under the cover of the dry shrubs, hoping the sound of his movement was masked by the tire noise. Fortunately Tank had actually obeyed his stay command this time and remained with Heather, so he didn't have to worry about the dog darting in front of the car.

Bill chose a spot behind a massive overgrown alder with enough space through the branches for him to get a good look, but the moonlight was obscured by clouds, so he could catch only an indistinct profile.

He waited until the car stopped, a head poking out to examine the ground.

"Out of the car!" Bill shouted, moving from behind the cover and aiming at the dark head. "Now."

The driver obeyed.

Bill tensed as the door opened.

"It's me," Crow said as he climbed out of the vehicle, hands held in front of him.

Bill gaped, then lowered his weapon. "I almost shot you."

Crow grinned. "My wife has that urge sometimes, but so far she hasn't gone through with it."

Heather jogged up with the dogs in tow. She stopped when she saw Crow. "What are you doing here?"

Tank bounded over and nearly sent Crow sprawling. Choo Choo trotted up to get in on the action.

Crow jerked his chin at Bill. "If you'll get these dogs off me I'll tell you."

Bill ordered Tank to sit and, to his amusement, both dogs sank to the ground.

Crow shook his head. "I was checking the perimeter, is all. Wanted to see if Oscar was prowling around. You messaged me that you thought he was holing up in the caves."

Bill wished it was daylight so he could read Crow's face better. "So you're driving around here without telling anyone? With no lights?"

Crow laughed. "How else do you catch a predator?"

Bill ignored the gibe. "You didn't inform me or anyone else that you'd be here."

He shrugged. "I still live here. I can do what I want."

Bill eyed the car. "Not in your official car and not off reservation land."

"Look, Bill," Crow said, hands on hips, "I was just trying to help you find the guy who wants you dead. If that's a problem, I'll just get out of your way, but frankly, you're not doing so hot on your own, are you?"

"Seemed to me like you were looking for something on the ground."

"Looking for tire tracks, footprints. Some Lakota you are, Cloudman. No tracking skills left?"

"Better keep folks informed, Al."

"I'll just go and tell the Feds my every move. I'm sure they'll be real interested." He shot Bill a glance. "Guess you forget that you're not official anymore, are you? You give a lot of orders for a guy without a badge."

Bill didn't stop Crow as he returned to the car, started the engine and turned on the headlights. The SUV rattled off down the road.

"That was not what I expected from him," Heather said. "I thought you two were close."

He'd thought so, too, and Crow's words hurt more than he wanted to admit. "He was offended that I questioned him."

Heather patted both dogs. "I get the feeling you don't believe him."

"I've worked with Al for years and he's never given me reason not to trust him."

"Yes," she said, straightening. "But you've got that 'something's not right' tilt to your head."

He consciously straightened, chagrined that she could read him so easily. "At this point, I can count on one hand the number of people I trust."

The glimmer of moonlight caught her face, lighting the pools of her eyes and catching the curls that framed her face. He wished she was one of those people again. She knew him better than anyone, except maybe Aunt Jean. He would take a bullet for Heather without question.

But would he trust her with his heart one more time? The soft and unprotected place where memories of Leanne and Johnny lived, and the sweet remnants of days spent with her?

As much as he wanted to, he knew the answer was no.

"Let's get you back home. I'll keep watch until morning."

She hesitated, glancing at the house. He knew it took more courage for her to go back in there than he could ever imagine. Before he could think himself out of it, he put an arm around her shoulders and dropped a kiss on her temple.

She melted into him for one tender moment before she straightened, once again inserting the distance between them.

They got into the truck without any further conversation and he took her home.

* * *

The next morning Heather felt like a caged animal. Minutes passed agonizingly into hours. Monday. It was Monday.

One more day. The thought crawled through her mind with such insidious force that she thought she would go mad. As much as she tried to pass the time working and researching her next article, the thought kept returning.

Oscar would try to kill Bill tomorrow and there was nothing she could do about it.

Her mother had emerged just after lunch and now sat quietly in a chair reading. Heather didn't know what to do about that, either, after their extraordinary discussion the night before. She found herself darting surreptitious glances at her, as if she was some intriguing stranger.

Which she was, sort of.

Bill's words floated back into her mind. *I wanted to save you...because I loved you.*

But he wouldn't forgive her, any more than she could forgive her mother. Forgiveness. It was something she'd relied on to fight her way to sobriety—forgiveness from her father and those she'd hurt with her drinking. She'd needed it so badly, so why didn't she have the strength to give it? Or ask for it from the one person she'd really wounded?

Forgiveness was more precious than she'd ever realized, given so easily by Jesus but so reluctantly by His children. What was that verse? she wondered. Moved by a sudden strong need to know, she snatched up her father's worn Bible from the shelf and thumbed through until she found it in Matthew 18:22. Forgiveness should be given seventy times seven times, inexhaustibly granted to the one who honestly sought it.

It was divine, a reflection of God's abundant forgiveness of her own sins.

She looked at her mother again, slowly turning pages, methodical and precise.

There was a knock at the door and Heather sprang from her chair. Holding a finger to her lips she cautioned her mother to stay quiet.

Margot put down her book and took firm hold of her cane.

Heather peeked through the curtain and saw Rudley and Bill standing on the porch. She opened the door and noticed the third person. Tina Moon held Bill's hand.

"Hiya, Heather," Tina said.

Bill and Rudley ushered her inside and closed the door.

Heather watched in surprise as Bill led Tina to the sofa.

"We found her crossing the bridge to your property. She said she needed to tell you something."

Heather sat next to her, trying to keep the anxiety out of her voice. "Okay. Tell me."

Tina scratched her knee, looking around. "Who's that?" she asked, pointing a finger at Margot.

"That's my...mother," Heather said.

"Oh. You're lucky. I don't got one anymore."

Heather opened her mouth and closed it again. She didn't have one, either, really. Did she?

Bill crouched next to Tina. "Honey, we need you to tell Heather your message, please, so we can get you back home. It's not safe for you to be walking around outside."

Tina's brown eyes widened. "'Cuz of the monster?"

Bill looked helplessly at Heather.

"There's a bad man in town," Heather said. "The police are going to find him but until they do, you need to stay inside. Okay?"

"Okay, but Uncle Charlie told me to come and get you."

"Me? Why?"

"'Cuz he can't get his legs to work."

A ripple of concern went through her. "Why didn't he call me?"

Tina shrugged. "His cell phone is dead and he can't reach the one on the wall."

Heather's gaze moved to Bill, whose eyes revealed a mixture of worry and suspicion.

Rudley was already moving to the door, talking into his radio. "We'll go check it out. Stay here."

"I want to go," Tina said, suddenly tearful. "Uncle Charlie said to come back right away. I want to go."

Bill and Rudley didn't slow. "We'll be back for you in a few minutes," Bill said.

Tina jumped from the couch and ran, wrapping her arms around Bill's leg. "No, I want to go home. Take me back to Uncle Charlie."

Heather was so startled by the look of pain on Bill's face that she couldn't answer for a moment.

To her surprise, her mother did.

"I've got an idea," Margot announced, climbing to her feet. "Tina, since you've come all this way, I would like to show you my collection of shells and fossils. I think I even have a jewel in my treasure box."

Tina sniffed. "You got a treasure box?"

Margot nodded, face serious. "Yes. Do you collect treasures, too?"

"Uh-huh." She let go of Bill's leg and stuck her small hand into her pocket and shook it. "Got 'em here and some at home."

"Okay, then. Let's go have a look at our treasures." Margot gestured to Heather. "I believe I saw your stash of chocolate bars in the cupboard. Chocolate goes well with treasure sorting."

Tina followed Margot and they shuffled down the hallway. She felt Bill's hand on her shoulder and realized her mouth was hanging open. He squeezed. "Be right back. There's a Tribal Ranger in front in case of any trouble. Lock up."

The door closed behind him.

Mechanically she went to fasten the bolt.

What had just happened? She'd seen her mother behaving like…a mother. Had it been like that when Heather was little? She found herself pacing in small circles. She should be angry to see those maternal qualities bestowed on a child who wasn't even hers. She should be angry, but she wasn't.

For some reason she felt filled with wonder, as if she'd stepped from a dark room into a dazzling explosion of sunlight. She shook her head but the feeling didn't clear away, so she fetched the chocolate bars and delivered them to the next room.

Margot and Tina sat at either end of the little table in the guest room, solemnly looking at the odds and ends that Tina pulled one at a time from her pocket. Margot commented about each one.

"That's a good sample of quartzite," she said. "Let's put it here with the metamorphic rocks."

"What's that?" Tina said, chewing a strand of hair.

Heather winced inwardly, knowing her mother was about to let loose with a river of scientific terms that would go completely over Tina's head.

"Metamorphic rock is made underground where there is a lot of heat and heaviness to press it together." She shot Heather a look. "I remember explaining this same thing to you."

Their eyes met and Heather allowed herself a smile, which her mother returned. "I'm sure I wasn't as good a student as Tina."

Margot laughed. "You had just as many trinkets in your pockets. We had to have a category for plastics and candy in your collection."

Heather felt her eyes fill and escaped to the kitchen before the tears streamed down. "What is the matter with me?" She splashed some cold water on her face and took a few deep breaths.

Focus on what's important here. She glanced at the calendar. One more day. What was Bill walking into on Charlie's property? Was the whole thing some sort of ruse cooked up to lure him over there?

She imagined him tripping an explosive, just as Johnny had, or being shot in the back as he approached the house. She didn't trust Oscar not to abandon his deadline. The man was a lunatic.

And what of Charlie Moon? He was the only family Tina had left. What would happen to her if he was taken out of the picture? Oscar would not hesitate to kill people for his own purposes, as he had with poor Mr. Brown.

The tension twirled around inside as she paced the carpet.

It was not fair that Oscar might win. How many people did Bill have to lose? His partner? His sister?

The thought popped up before she could stop it.

Me.

I'm sorry, Bill. I'm sorry I hurt you. She wondered if she would ever have the chance to tell him.

Even though he might never be able to forgive her.

Thoughts tumbled faster and faster through her mind. She tried to make some sense of the situation, to find in the madness some kernel that might help Bill crack the case before Oscar won. She could not shake the feeling that there was something to be learned from Hazel's death. The photo of the open car door, the broken lipstick on the ground, but no purse. And what had Oscar said on the bridge?

His wife and a woman. He'd alluded to a woman whose death he'd blamed on Bill, as well.

Another memory poked at her—Al Crow, Bill's longtime friend and colleague whom she'd found to be closemouthed and hostile when she'd asked him about Hazel's purse. But he couldn't have anything to do with the situation. Bill had known him since before he was partnered with Johnny. Her pacing became faster until she was nearly jogging around the small family room. A sound sent her running to the window.

She peeked through the curtains in time to see Bill returning. Her body relaxed. It hadn't been a trap. This time.

She opened the door and he came in, looking tired and worn. She was so filled with relief that she threw her arms around him, pressing her face to the place where the pulse pounded in his neck. "I thought it was Oscar. I thought…"

He clutched her to him, tightly, convulsively, moving his cheek along the top of her head, his hands sending tingles along her back where he stroked her. "I'm okay."

She found herself wanting that embrace to last forever, to keep him wound tightly in the circle of her arms where the memories and dangers could not intrude. Instead he exhaled a deep and shuddering breath and pulled her to arm's length.

"Where's Tina?"

She swallowed, trying to calm her racing heart. "In the back with my mother. What happened over there? What did you find?"

"I've got some news," he said, his face grim. "And it's not the good kind."

FOURTEEN

Bill walked to the window and looked out to give himself a moment to find his balance again. He felt the lingering electricity shooting through him from Heather's embrace. The touch fired sparks inside that seemed to blast away the numbing cloud that had surrounded him since she'd left.

Please don't let her come close to me again.

He wondered who he was speaking to until it dawned on him with brutal clarity. He was speaking to God. Fingering the curtains, he gritted his teeth. Enough of that. God was not in charge. Bill would keep Heather away until his showdown with Oscar. No heavenly help required.

But what about after?

He flicked the curtain closed.

There would be no "after" for them.

He would have his vengeance and she would get her life back. End of story. He would put away the happy memories of her to be savored and enjoyed in solitude. Above all things, he would not put what was left of his heart out to be battered again.

Heather watched him, mouth drawn in concern, eyes wide. "What happened?"

"We found Charlie unconscious. He's had some sort of medical problem. Rudley's got an ambulance coming."

"Are you sure Oscar didn't get to him?"

He sighed. "Not sure of anything, but there was no sign of violence. Oscar would have no reason to go after Charlie. It appears he might have had a stroke or fallen."

Heather sank onto the sofa. "Oh, no. Is it really bad?"

"He's alive and breathing on his own, but we couldn't rouse him. Doctors will have to tell us more."

She groaned. "Charlie's all Tina's got. Where will she go?"

Bill considered the question that had been alive in his mind since the day Johnny died. What would happen to Tina with only an old man to care for her? Johnny had never forgotten a birthday, never skipped a chance to play in the river with Tina. He'd been mother and father to her with Charlie's help, and his death left an old grieving man to fill the void. A swell of desperation engulfed Bill.

He was still wrestling with the problem when he felt Heather's hand on his forearm.

"She can stay here with us. Mom and I will do our best until we can figure something else out."

He sighed. It was a generous offer, considering Heather's uncertain relationship with her own mother. "Thank you, but I think she'd be safer with Aunt Jean for a little while. I already phoned her."

"Why would she be safer at Jean's? Oscar's been there, too."

"Yes, but I think he's focused more on you." Bill turned and found himself so close that his arms seemed to encircle her of their own accord, as if his body was no longer ruled by his mind. Her eyes sought his, filled with such tender compassion that he found it hard to breathe. He desperately wanted to press his mouth to hers and drink in some of the warmth that filled her heart and soul. "I'm sorry for that, for all of it."

She reached up and put her palm gently on his cheek. He

longed to press against it, to dive into that touch and let the
world go away.

"You're not responsible for Oscar's craziness. You never
have been." She added softly, "And you're not responsible for
what he did to Johnny."

He wanted to believe it, but laying down that burden of
responsibility even for a moment would leave his heart open
to moving on. To what? To love again? To turn back to the
life he'd had before and the faith he'd left behind? It was too
much.

He allowed himself to linger for another moment in the
warmth of her touch and then he moved away. Tomorrow. It
would all be over one way or another tomorrow.

Out the window he could see the ambulance had arrived
and begun to load Charlie onto a stretcher. Heather joined
him and they watched until the rescue vehicle departed.

He cleared his throat, dreading the news he would have to
give Tina. He wasn't good with kids. He could hardly even
get Tank to listen. What chance did he have with a precocious
six-year-old? "Would you come with me to Charlie's? I've got
to take her back so she can pack up a few things she'll need.
I'm not sure how she's going to handle this." *And I'm not sure
how to handle it, either.*

"Of course. I'll go get her."

Trying to piece together what to tell Tina, Bill waited until
they entered the room.

Tina climbed up and sat next to Heather on the sofa. "Am
I going home now, Uncle Bill? I'm not done sorting my treasures."

Margot gave her a smile. "Don't worry. I'll take care of
them until you can come over again and we'll finish."

The girl seemed satisfied. "Is Uncle Charlie better now?"

Bill swallowed. "Honey, Uncle Charlie has to go to the
hospital for a while."

Tina stuck her fingers in her mouth. "Is he gonna come back?"

The pain knifed at him. He knew she was remembering that Johnny never returned from the hospital.

Tina's eyes began to tear up and he took a step toward her, unable to find even a single word to comfort her.

Heather took Tina's free hand. "The doctors are going to take very good care of him."

Tina clutched at Heather, her words garbled from the fingers jammed into her mouth. "Is he gonna die? I don't want him to die."

Heather stroked Tina's arm. "I know you feel scared. Do you know what I do when I'm really scared?"

Tina shook her head.

"I pray to God. Do you know how to do that?"

She nodded. "Aunt Jean taught me."

"Okay. Let's say a prayer together, then."

Bill watched them, heads bent together as Heather guided the little girl through a simple prayer. He ached at the sight. How could she trust God after she'd lost so much? How could they both commend Charlie into His care in spite of the grief they had both experienced?

But when they looked up, both had the same childlike peace about them, as if they had put down a heavy burden. Heather's eyes found his and he knew she could see the yearning on his face. He looked away.

"Aunt Jean is going to take care of you for a while. I'll walk you home to pack up some things to bring along, okay?" Heather said.

Tina nodded, fingers still in her mouth, as she hopped off the sofa.

Bill cleared his throat. "Thank you," he said to Heather. "For helping her with that."

Heather smiled. "I've had a lot of experience feeling like an overwhelmed child. Still do, sometimes."

He didn't reply as they walked outside, checking the perimeter as they did so, nodding to the Tribal Ranger still stationed at the front. Both dogs joined them, sniffing and nosing their way along onto Charlie's property, where they were left to explore outside.

Rudley clicked off his phone and greeted them at the door. Tina shuffled past him down the hallway, which was piled with cardboard boxes. "Got someone going to check Aunt Jean's place again to make sure everything is normal before I transport Tina over there."

"I'll take her," Bill snapped. "She needs someone familiar."

Rudley shook his head. "Not you."

"I…" Bill stopped. Rudley was right.

I'm a target and everywhere I go I put the people with me in danger.

Heather must have sensed his thoughts. "I'll go with you, Agent Rudley. Tina knows me a little. I'll help her get settled with Aunt Jean."

Bill felt a surge of gratefulness that left him unsteady. He walked into the tiny front room, noting more boxes stacked against the wall. Moving boxes. Charlie must have found a buyer, or at least a renter, for his land and was going to follow through on his goal to get Tina out of South Dakota. Where would they go? Someplace, anyplace where memories of Johnny did not linger in every dusty canyon or under the shade of each cottonwood tree.

It wouldn't work, he thought grimly. The memories would follow along. He thought of Leanne, chasing her through endless acres of crackling golden grass, helping her deliver pizzas to make ends meet. The birth of her daughters, his nieces, and the joy on her face, in spite of the fact that the man who fathered them had taken off long before they were born.

Heather followed Tina down the hall, to help her pack, he imagined. Rudley began texting, leaving Bill to wander among the boxes. The house was dingy, he noticed, the paint peeling along the baseboards, the worn carpeting stained and threadbare. For Johnny it was an endless task to repair this old place, a job Bill had never once heard him complain about.

The question returned. Who would have bought this house? Or even be interested in renting it? Rockvale had suffered the full brunt of the economic downturn, in addition to the poverty that seemed an integral part of life on the nearby Eagle Rock reservation. People did not come to Rockvale, except for the lab folks, and they lived in housing constructed specifically for that purpose in Copper Springs, a nearby town with better amenities and a bigger population.

So who had bought this place?

He was still musing when Heather and Tina came into the room, Tina holding a duffel bag.

"All packed," Heather said brightly.

A glint of metal caught Bill's eye and he looked closer at Tina, at something she was wearing around her neck. As he got a good look, he grunted in surprise, not believing what he saw.

Heather saw Bill's face go slack with shock as he darted toward Tina and dropped to one knee. Reflexively she grabbed the little girl's hand. "What is it? What's wrong?"

Bill ignored her. He reached up and put one finger on the silver heart that hung on a chain around Tina's neck. "Where did you get that?"

Tina shrank back and put her fingers into her mouth again with a shrug of her slender shoulders.

His voice cracked as he repeated the question, causing Tina to hide behind Heather. She whispered to him.

"You're scaring her."

He remained on the floor for a moment before he stood again and backed away a few steps, but she could see the emotion storming through his eyes.

"The necklace. I need to know where she got it."

Heather did not understand what was driving Bill, but she knew him well enough to know he didn't ruffle easily. Whatever the reason for his interest in the necklace, it was serious.

"Tina," she said. "Uncle Bill was surprised to see your pretty necklace. Can you tell him who gave it to you?"

Tina shook her head, so Heather led her to a chair and sat next to her. "It's important. Uncle Bill isn't mad at you. He just needs to know, okay?"

Tina had a fearful expression on her face as she looked from Bill to Heather.

"I found it," she finally said. "On the other side of the bridge."

Heather frowned. The other side of the bridge would be her father's land, but the necklace was nothing she had ever seen before.

"How long ago?" Bill croaked.

Tina screwed up her face in thought. "A long time ago. The same time I started to go take art class at Aunt Jean's."

"Last September," Bill said. "You found the necklace in September."

Rudley was listening in now, having caught the tension.

Heather watched Bill take a steadying breath.

"Did you find anything else with the necklace, honey?" he asked.

She stared at her lap. Bill touched the top of her head very gently. "It's real important. I promise you won't get in trouble if you tell the truth."

Tina looked at Rudley, eyes narrowed.

Heather patted her hand. "Agent Rudley won't punish you, either, right?"

Rudley looked bemused. "Oh, of course not. We never punish children."

Tina seemed satisfied. "I'll get it." She hopped off the chair and disappeared down the hallway.

Bill remained frozen there and his strange behavior scared Heather. She wanted to grab his shoulders and shake the wild, faraway look off his face, but she didn't dare. Instead she watched, holding her breath until Tina returned with a grimy brown purse.

It was made of cheap vinyl and one of the handles was almost severed. The outside was pocked with dings as if it had been badly treated.

She handed it to Bill. "Uncle Charlie doesn't like me to collect treasures, so I hid it in my room."

Bill took the purse, frowning, and carefully slid the contents out onto the table. A compact, the one Heather had seen Tina powdering her nose with before, a curved white rock, a mint container and a wallet.

The wallet was empty except for a dirty driver's license. Heather itched to examine it, but Rudley and Bill moved in. All was quiet until Rudley let out a low whistle.

Heather couldn't take a moment longer. "What? Tell me before I have to scream."

Rudley was pulling out his phone. "It's Hazel Birch's purse."

"Hazel? Oscar's wife?" Suddenly the mystery of the missing purse was solved. She was right. Hazel *had* grabbed her purse before she fled, before Oscar caught up and murdered her. "But why would Oscar dump his wife's purse on my property?"

"There's another mystery here," Bill said, voice dull. They all turned to stare at him.

"That necklace. Turn it over and read the back."

With fingers suddenly gone cold, Heather turned over the heart on the chain around Tina's neck.

"It says, 'To Leanne…'" She broke off.

Bill filled in the rest. "'The new mother. Love, Bill.'"

Heather stared at him in horror. "This was your sister's."

He nodded. "I gave it to her on the day her girls were born. She never took it off."

"Then how…?"

Rudley spoke softly. "It would seem that Hazel knew something about Leanne's death. She found the necklace, some other evidence perhaps that Oscar was involved."

"But I thought…" Heather flushed. "I thought Leanne died of a drug overdose."

"She did," Bill growled. "But it might not have been self-induced, after all."

Rudley nodded. "Hazel guessed Oscar was involved and decided to run, but Oscar caught her."

She saw from the white-hot rage kindling in Bill's eyes that he agreed with Rudley's theory.

"But how did the purse get here?" she finally managed.

"I think I know the answer to that, too," he said as he stalked out the front door.

FIFTEEN

He didn't have to go far. Al Crow was pulling up the gravel drive. Bill waited for him to get out, fury building to a crescendo inside him.

Al gave him a curious look. "What's up? You look like you're about to explode."

Heather and Rudley jogged up next to them.

"What's going on?" Rudley asked.

"Why don't you tell him what you did?" Bill snapped at Crow.

"I don't know what you're talking about."

"Yes, you do. Last September you found the car Hazel Birch abandoned before Oscar killed her."

Crow shifted, arms crossed. "There's a whole report on file about that. I don't see why we gotta talk about it now."

The rage overwhelmed him and he grabbed Crow by the collar. "How could you do it?"

Crow struggled in his grasp until Rudley pulled him away. Heather clamped a hand on Bill's shoulder.

"Calm down. Calm down and tell us," she said in a soothing voice.

Bill tried to suck in some air. His heart hammered an angry rhythm against his ribs. "Hazel found out that Oscar killed my sister."

Crow's face blanched. "What? But Leanne died of an O.D. I thought...."

"That's what we all thought, thanks to the blood tests, but now it seems like Oscar just made it look that way. Maybe somehow he overpowered her and injected her with the stuff and pushed her body off the ridge. We don't know for sure, but we *do* know he took her necklace first." He looked out at the distant edge of Charlie's property, the place where he imagined Oscar had taken Leanne's life. "Hazel had the necklace in her purse. Somehow she found it, guessed that Oscar killed Leanne and was going to tell, but he caught her."

Crow licked his lips. "How do you know that?"

Rudley spoke up. "Tina just showed us Hazel's purse. She found it, with the necklace inside, on the Fernandes property last September."

"Someone," Bill said, fighting the urge to grab Crow around the neck, "took the purse from her car and didn't want to be caught with it, so they discarded it on Heather's land. That someone was you, wasn't it?"

He heard Heather gasp but he did not take his eyes off Crow. "Why did you do it, Al?" The rage suddenly drained out of him and he felt unaccountably fatigued. "Why didn't you report the purse?"

Crow looked down at his feet. "I made a mistake."

"Why?" Bill said, though he knew the answer already.

"I needed the money. I have some debts."

Bill shook his head. "That's why you sold your Falcon?"

He nodded. "It was stupid, but when I found that purse there and a wallet with a couple hundred bucks..."

"You took it?" Heather's voice was incredulous.

"Yeah. I was first on scene sitting in my vehicle. At that time I had no idea it was a murder investigation. All I knew is it was an abandoned car, so I looked through the wallet. Then I heard Cloudman and Johnny approaching. I panicked. I hid the purse in my car. By the time it was clear we were look-ing for Hazel and it wasn't going to turn out well, I'd already told Bill and Johnny there was no purse, so I couldn't put it back. Later I dumped the purse at Heather's."

Bill pushed on. "You meant to go back and get it later."

"Yeah, but it was gone. After a few months went by, I stopped looking, but when Oscar showed up and there were all kinds of cops roaming over Heather's land, I figured I'd better find it before they did, on the off chance it was still there."

Heather edged closer. "So it was you on my property with the lantern? You swung a shovel at Bill?"

He looked confused. "No. That wasn't me. I wouldn't have done that to Bill."

"What you did was worse." Bill's eyes burned. "You con-cealed evidence that would have told me that Oscar murdered my sister. All this time I thought she caved in and started using again. All this time—" He broke off.

Crow seemed to shrink. "I'm sorry, Bill. I had no idea there was a connection between Hazel and Leanne. I never would have kept it from you."

"You kept it from all of us and you kept my sister from having justice. Because of you her daughters think their mother died a junkie."

Crow's mouth opened and then closed.

Rudley exhaled. "Crow, you'd better come with me. I'll make arrangements with you to talk to someone at head-quarters." He turned to Bill and spoke more gently. "We can exhume your sister's body and have a thorough postmortem. We'll talk it out in a little while."

Bill walked away in disgust. Talk? What good was that now? His friend, his longtime friend, had betrayed him. Crow might face the loss of his badge, his career, but Bill had lost so much more. The bitterness almost overwhelmed him. Vaguely

he noticed Tina trot out the door to play with the two dogs. He
sank onto a worn bench under the shade of a scraggly pine,
head reeling.

He felt rather than saw Heather sit next to him. "I'm sorry,"
she said.

"I should have believed in her. She said she was clean and
I should have known she was telling me the truth. I never
should have believed she overdosed."

Heather reached out and took his hand. "Speaking from
experience, an addiction problem destroys trust so completely,
it's hard to win it back, no matter how much you try."

"Her girls, her children." The thought made his throat
thicken. "They think she was a failure."

"You can tell them the truth."

He laughed bitterly. "I don't even know where Rose is.
She's been in and out of trouble for so long we've lost track
of her. It might be too late."

"You'll find her, I know you will. I'll help you."

He closed his eyes. "That day, the day I found you driving drunk. You asked me to let you off, you begged me and
I wanted to. I wanted to turn my back and forget it ever happened, but I couldn't."

He opened his eyes and gripped her hand. "You know why
I didn't."

Heather nodded, lips trembling. "Because you loved me
and you didn't want me to turn out like your sister."

For a moment he could not form any words. "I wanted you
to get help before it was too late. That's why I arrested you.
That's why I called and emailed."

She was weeping now. "But I didn't answer because I was
too ashamed. It was wrong. I know now why you did what
you did and I'm sorry. I'm terribly, terribly sorry, Bill."

Part of him wanted to comfort her, but he could summon
up no gentle feelings inside to offer. He put his head in his

hands. "All this time I've blamed myself for Johnny's death and now I find out my sister was murdered right under my nose, too."

She caressed his face, her own wet with tears. "Bill, stop. You can't shoulder all this blame."

The words flowed out faster and faster. "The day we finally cornered Oscar, I was calling for backup but Johnny didn't wait. He ran in when it should have been me."

"No, Bill."

"He went in because he knew I wasn't at the top of my game. I wasn't sleeping, or eating well since you left. He went in because he thought it would protect me somehow, when I should have been the one looking out for him."

She caught hold of his other hand. "You've got to forgive yourself."

"No, I don't." He pulled away and stood, gesturing to Tina. "Look at that little girl with no brother to watch over her. No parents. My nieces have no mother to come home to. Don't talk to me about forgiveness."

"When we knew each other before, you used to give your burdens to God, remember?" She moved to him, arms raised to embrace him. "Bill, He's still there for you, if you'll let Him in."

He fixed his eyes on the rocky cliff that stood stalwart and alone against the brilliant sky. "I'm not going to let anyone in, Heather. Ever again."

Heather watched in despair as an impassive mask settled into place on Bill's face. Leanne's murder was the final shovelful of earth that buried Bill under a massive weight of grief and guilt. He walked away, and leaned against the split rail fence. Suddenly she realized how hard it must have been for him to love her in the first place.

The moments together when he'd let his guard down, his

bumbling attempts to learn to cook for her, the places he'd shown her that were precious to him because he and his sister had played there as children. Each of those moments was an act of faith in her and in God. Now it was all gone. She realized there were tears coursing down her face and she wiped them away with her sleeve, surprised to see her mother and Dr. Egan walking over the bridge toward them.

Dr. Egan looked from Heather to Bill. "I came to deliver the water sample results to Margot. Everything's clean. I thought it might help with the investigation in some way."

Bill rounded on him. "What made you think my sister was using?"

Egan took a step back at the ferocity in Bill's voice. "Why do you ask?"

"Because we've just uncovered evidence that suggests she was murdered by Oscar Birch," Heather said.

Egan's mouth dropped open and Heather would have laughed at his comical expression under different circumstances.

"Murdered? How could that be?"

"Just answer the question," Bill barked.

Egan still did not speak, his face white. Margot patted him on the shoulder. "What kind of behaviors was she showing that made you concerned?"

Heather was grateful for her mother's calm intervention. She was afraid to leave Bill's side in case he went after Egan as he had Al Crow.

Egan wiped a hand over his brow. "I met her when we arranged to have pizza brought in for the lab employees one day. She was very friendly, offered to show us around the town. Pizza lunches became a regular treat at the lab, so we got to know your sister. When the custodial job came up, I recommended her. She was always on time, always cheerful until a few weeks before her death. She came in late, looked pale and haggard." He looked to Bill. "You must have noticed, surely."

Bill flushed and then looked at the ground. "I didn't."

She saw it in his face. The terrible guilt.

"But it could be that Leanne wasn't using at all. Oscar killed her and made it look like an overdose," Heather suggested.

Egan shook his head and she saw moisture gleaming in his eyes. "Leanne was a sweet lady. She reminded me of my daughter. Angie lived with her mother since she was a little girl. I never saw her much." His face fell. "But I remember her being like that, very open and full of life." He seemed to snap out of his recollections. "Whether Leanne died from drugs or Oscar Birch, I wish I could have done something to help. Mr. Cloudman, all I can say is if there was anything I should have noticed that would have saved your sister and I missed it, I am sincerely sorry."

Bill remained silent.

Heather spoke to her mother. "When Rudley gets back I'm going to go with him over to Aunt Jean's and get Tina settled in there. Her uncle's going to be in the hospital for a while."

Margot nodded. "I'll go, too." She held up a bag. "I brought the rest of her treasures along. We could finish sorting them on the way." She looked suddenly anxious. "Unless she is too worried about her uncle. Do you think that's the right thing to do?"

Heather looked at her mother, noticing how the fully risen sun etched her face with a delicate web of wrinkles. Her heart swelled a little. "Yes, Mom. I think that's exactly the right thing to do."

Margot stood there for a moment, bag held up in her fingers. "Good. That's what we'll do, then," she said, her gaze lingering on Heather's face.

Heather walked Choo Choo back to her house, closing him

in securely before she returned to Charlie's property, noticing that both Bill and the officer stationed in her front yard kept a close eye on her the entire time.

She thought of Oscar. Her skin chilled as she crossed the small bridge. Was he there now? Watching them? Waiting for the minutes to tick by? If Oscar succeeded he would have accomplished five murders; his own wife, Johnny, possibly Leanne, Mr. Brown…and Bill.

The only way Oscar could win was if he murdered Bill, too. Oscar's words tumbled through her memory.

Tell him I'll be seeing him soon.

The phone in Heather's pocket vibrated and she jumped and almost dropped it.

"Honey." The low voice rumbled through the phone. "I got the new number you left on my voice mail. Did you upgrade to one of those fancy phones?"

She blinked back tears. "Hi, Dad. Nah, just a loaner because mine…broke." Walking away a few paces, she sought the shade of the pine while her father filled her in.

"Sorry I didn't call sooner. One of my guys was injured and I've been at the hospital with him. Couldn't use my cell much and I forgot my charger. Looks like they've got him all patched up. How are things there?"

How were things? With Oscar's deadline approaching? Charlie in the hospital? And evidence of Leanne's murder surfacing? Things couldn't be worse, but she would not worry her father by explaining. Besides, she knew what he was really asking. "Mom got here safely. She's doing okay."

"I'm sorry about all that. I didn't mean to surprise you. It just sort of came up, but it wasn't fair to spring her on you without warning. Are you two hanging in there?"

"I don't know, Dad. I always wanted her to come back, but now that she's here, I'm all confused. Sometimes I am so mad at her I can't take it another moment, and other times…"

Her father laughed. "I've felt that way quite often myself."

Heather pictured his smile. "How can you take it, then?"

"Honey, I just remind myself that God's the ultimate handyman. He can fix anything, if we let Him."

She glanced at Bill, head bowed, anguish written in the lines of his body. Would Bill ever allow his heart to be fixed? Sorrow swirled inside her, but she forced herself to keep a cheerful tone for her father's sake.

"Are you sure everything is all right there?" he asked. "You sound strange."

"It's fine, Dad. I can't wait to see you soon." How would things be when the three of them were together under one roof?

He promised he'd be home in another three weeks.

She said goodbye, wondering what news she'd have to give her father when he arrived.

SIXTEEN

It was hours before Rudley returned to take Tina to Aunt Jean's. Egan and Margot waited in the shade, talking quietly about geological topics Bill had never heard of. Heather played with Tina and Tank, watching Bill from the corner of her eye when she thought he wasn't looking.

His heart felt like a hardened lump in his chest. All he could think about was Leanne. She might have had a shot at a normal life, a steady job, two children who could have reconnected with her someday. All the time, he had thought he'd let her down by not noticing her drug abuse. Now he realized he'd been feeling guilty for the wrong thing; Oscar Birch had taken her life, right under Bill's nose, and he'd never suspected it because deep down he believed his sister would fail.

Deep down he always knew or feared she would start using again.

And maybe deep down he believed the same about Heather.

Oh, God, help me.

He didn't know what he needed help with. Forgiving Heather? Forgiving himself for not trusting Leanne? He wanted some warm feeling, some tender comfort to latch on to, but he couldn't see anything but blackness.

There was only one thing left to accomplish that meant anything.

Bringing down Oscar Birch.

Rudley helped put Tina's bag in the car and approached Bill. "Crow will be suspended pending investigation."

Bill nodded. It could not be any other way; the man was no longer trustworthy as an officer. Still, Bill felt both angered and sorry. What would Crow do now without his badge? Bill knew firsthand what it felt like to be adrift without a career and only regrets and shame to fill up the days.

Heather took a few hesitant steps toward him but he turned away, his mind too full of despair to risk a conversation with her. He heard the motor start up and watched them drive off.

Egan stood on the small bridge, looking down at the spot where only a dry gulley was carved into the earth by long-ago rains, without appearing to see it. Bill did not want to speak to him, but he found himself drawing close anyway, while Tank bounded down into the dry chasm after a squirrel.

Bill cleared his throat. "Dr. Egan?"

Egan looked up, startled. "I thought you would go with them."

"No. They're better off without me." Both men looked into the creek bed, now filling with dust as Tank raced through it. "I apologize," Bill said, surprised at his own words.

Egan continued to stare down at the creek.

"I blamed you for not telling me about Leanne's drug abuse, but there may not have been anything to tell. You were good to her, got her a job and all." He picked up a leaf that landed on the wood rail and tore it up. "Anyway, I just wanted to say that."

Egan turned to him, his face pained. "Thank you. I know that must have been hard for you to say."

Bill nodded.

"So what will you do now?"

"Find Oscar Birch."

"And kill him before he kills you?" Egan's eyes locked on Bill's.

Bill checked his watch. "Almost five. I think I'd better get out of here." He didn't want to be anywhere near Heather as Oscar's deadline approached. "I'll walk you back to your car."

Egan stuck his hands in his pockets as they headed back. "Don't blame yourself too much, Mr. Cloudman, for thinking your sister was using. Sometimes people get in over their heads and one small choice ensnares them."

The heavy weight in Bill's chest felt as if it would sink him into the ground. One small choice. Heather's choice to start drinking to dull the pain of her mother's abandonment. His choice to arrest her. His decision long ago to pursue Oscar Birch up into the hills. The thoughts all whirled together in his mind, so he didn't notice Egan had stopped walking until Tank barked.

He jerked from his reverie. Egan stood on the dusty path. "Mr. Cloudman, you aren't going to believe this, but I think I just figured out where Oscar Birch might be hiding."

Bill's breath caught. "Tell me."

"When I came here five years ago, the lab had just broken ground. They picked out a site to house the construction equipment. It's outside the fenced perimeter, well off the main road. It's no more than a small warehouse, really, and it's completely abandoned."

"Why do you think he might be there?"

Egan's eyes darted in thought. "Because I like to hike at night sometimes. It allows me to see angles and geological deposits that I might not see in the daytime. I was hiking a week or so ago and I thought..." He trailed off.

"What? You thought what?"

"I thought I heard a humming noise coming from that area. I moved in closer to check, but I couldn't see anything and the noise stopped suddenly."

"A humming noise, like the kind made by a generator?"

Egan's eyes widened. "Exactly."

Finally. This time Oscar would be surprised. "Do you think you could show me the spot?"

Egan nodded. "Without a doubt."

Heather sat in the back of Rudley's car next to Tina. Her mother was in front chatting to Rudley, who looked as if he would rather be anyplace else. Tina's pockets bulged and she fished out a length of string and some bright pink beads, which she began to slide onto the string.

"What are you making?"

"A leash for Tank."

Heather hid a smile, picturing the enormous dog trotting along at the end of a pink beaded leash. Her thoughts turned back to Bill and the impenetrable anguish that had settled over him with news of his sister's murder. And all the time the evidence of that murder had been right next door, hidden among Tina's baubles.

"Would you please stop at the post office, Agent Rudley?" Margot said. "I need to pick something up and I believe it closes at six."

Rudley looked exasperated. "Can't it wait?"

"No," Margot said, calmly. "I don't think so."

"It's that important?" he asked.

"It is to me."

He sighed and pulled over at the post office, where Margot got out and made her way inside. Rudley sat, engine running, fingers drumming on the steering wheel.

Tina had strung more than twenty beads on her string,

when the knot at the end gave out, sending the beads sliding all over the floor.

Tina threw the string down in frustration. "It always breaks. Everything breaks," she wailed.

"We can fix it," Heather said, hurriedly scooping up the beads as her mother got back into the car, pocketing a white envelope.

"No," Tina said, sticking her fingers into her mouth. "No more."

Heather exchanged a look with her mother. Tina was not crying about the beads but about the frustration and fear she felt, which was too much for a child to express. Heather was not sure what to say, so she settled for scooping up the pink beads and putting them into her own pocket. "We can fix it later. I'll bet Aunt Jean will help."

Tina did not answer. She turned her face to the window and stared out at the cars coming and going from the post office parking lot.

Heather gave her mother a questioning "what should we do?" shrug, but her mother looked just as perplexed as Heather felt. She remembered with a jolt that her mother hadn't been there for much of the difficult parenting, so she probably had even fewer tools to fall back on than Heather had.

She was still struggling with trying to coax the child to talk when Rudley asked, "Have we got everything we need now?"

Margot favored him with a serene smile. "Yes, thank you. That didn't take very long, did it?"

Rudley didn't answer, but took off quickly out of the lot.

Heather wondered about the subject of the papers her mother had taken out of her pocket to peruse. She could not imagine what would be so important that it would completely absorb her mother for the next few miles, but it did exactly that.

The car was oppressively silent.

Rudley drove at a good clip away from town and toward the reservation. Heather closed her eyes and laid her head back against the seat. She hadn't realized how exhausted she was, but now the fatigue almost overwhelmed her. Dusk was upon them. The temperature was warm in spite of the air conditioner.

It made her remember a fall day when Bill had taken her to hike along Fox Creek, a scooped-out section between an upland plain and soaring cliffs on the other side. On the dry edge of the white-clay creek bed she'd found an enormous black boulder shattered into fragments. She'd picked up a piece, surprised to find it was dense and porous like an old slate blackboard. Bill had told her it was shale, rock formed from the decayed matter and disintegrated rocks of what had once been the bottom of the sea.

She hadn't told him she already knew it, a fact remembered from some long-ago conversation with her mother that she barely recalled.

She had stood there holding evidence in her hands that that dry place had once been an ancient sea. It had struck her then how sad it was that her mother, the one person she knew who could appreciate the meaning of that dull rock, was gone, leaving some of her own interests and passions buried deep inside her unwanted daughter. She had stood there for a long time, holding that rock, until she had felt Bill's hand on her shoulder.

"Tell me what you're thinking."

He had wanted her to share, to expose that vulnerable wound, to trust him with her most delicate feelings.

"Just a rock," she had said, tossing it away.

And later, she'd drowned the feelings in one drink after another.

If she had trusted him then, would he have helped her with her addiction?

She squeezed her eyes closed to hold in the tears.

It was too late to wonder.

Too late.

A sudden bang roused her. It felt as if something had struck the car. Her eyes flew open. She heard her mother gasp. Out the window she saw a large boulder still moving from impacting the driver's door.

Rudley turned, face deadly serious. "Get down."

"What? Why?" Heather gasped.

"Just…" He didn't get to finish the sentence before a bullet shattered the front window, passing between Rudley and Margot and blowing a hole in the backseat, so close Heather could feel it cut through the air. Bits of glass showered down around them.

She grabbed Tina and pulled her down.

Rudley swore as he stomped on the gas, and the car lurched forward. He yelled something over the squealing tires.

Heather screamed as the driver's side window suddenly exploded and Rudley crumpled, a red stain appearing on his temple. At first she couldn't understand what had happened.

"He's been shot," Margot screamed. The car continued to roll until it began to slide toward the sharp drop along the shoulder.

"Grab the wheel," Heather yelled at her mother.

In spite of her mother's frantic yanking, the car continued to slide until it toppled over the shoulder. Bumping violently, it gained speed until it crashed into a gnarled pine, halfway down the incline.

Fear galvanized her into action. She grabbed Tina and shoved at the door on the passenger side. At first it didn't open. With strength she hadn't realized she possessed, she shoved at the door until it gave and they tumbled out. Pushing

Tina along, all Heather could think of was getting away from that car, until she realized her mother was not following. She turned to find her still in the front seat, staring in round-eyed horror at Rudley.

She hammered on the door with her fist. "Unlock it, Mom."

Her mother didn't move, so she pounded against the window. "Mom, listen to me."

Her mother turned and seemed to waken.

"Unlock the door," Heather pleaded again.

When Margot lifted a trembling hand and unlocked it, Heather wrenched open the door, pulling her mother out.

"Run for the trees. We've got to get away."

They scrambled through brambles and shrubs, stumbling and sliding down the steep slope, not daring to look behind them as they ran. It was Oscar. Though she hadn't seen his face, she knew he'd been watching, waiting for the opportunity to use them to hurt Bill. Tina's face was white in the waning sunlight as Heather dragged her along, down, down, until they slithered to a stop where the land gave way to a flat ribbon of whitened soil that must have been a creek bed. A cliff rose on the other side, striated with dark bands of color. In both directions the dry creek twisted out of sight.

Which way?

Her heart pounded in her throat as she considered. She could not hear the sound of pursuit, but she knew Oscar would be after them any minute. Tina whimpered and Heather wanted to take the time to comfort her, but she didn't dare. She looked at her mother, who seemed to be in a state of shock.

"This way," she hissed at them, plunging toward a clump of aspen. "We've got to hide."

Her mother stumbled once and almost went down, but

Heather grabbed her elbow with her free hand. The three of them staggered along, feet slipping on the loose dry soil.

As they ran she could hear the sound of a car door. Had Rudley been able to get himself out of the car? Maybe Oscar had given up and driven away, rather than finish off a federal agent. She dismissed the thought.

Nothing would stop him.

And no obstacle would get in his way for very long.

Gripping Tina and her mother tighter, she practically hauled them to the shelter of the trees a hundred yards away, where they flopped to the ground, panting.

Tina's face was stark against the shade. She didn't speak, but terror was written clearly in her brown eyes.

Margot appeared calmer, but her limbs were shaking from either fear or the physical effort she'd just endured.

Heather knew she must be the one in charge if they were going to survive. Peeking past the trees, she saw that the way became rockier, littered with boulders that had broken from the cliffs above and come to settle in the creek. Small humps of white rock stood out against the darker sand and gravel here and there.

"Limestone."

She jerked, not realizing her mother had come to stand next to her.

Heather gave her mother an incredulous look. "Now is not the time for a geology lesson."

Her mother's lips quivered. "It's all I know. It's all I've ever known."

She recognized the helplessness on her mother's face. "It's okay. Do you have a cell phone, Mom?"

"No, I'm sorry."

Heather continued to scan the ever-darkening surroundings while she turned on her phone.

No signal. She felt like flinging it away in frustration, but instead she pocketed it.

Her mind pinwheeled, searching for escape routes. She could see only as far as the next bend. They could hide in one of the creek channels, or farther down in a clump of trees until help arrived. It might work, but not for long. The only real chance was the road, to flag down another car or get to a spot where she could call for help. With sickening clarity the answer dawned on her. She turned to face them.

"You two need to keep going, find a place to hide."

Margot's eyes widened. "What about you?"

"I'm going to head back the other way."

"Toward the car? Toward Oscar?"

She nodded. Her mother clamped a hand around her wrist.

"No. That won't do. We'll go together."

She stroked her mother's hand, feeling the delicate bones beneath the skin. She'd never thought of her mother as fragile or vulnerable until that very moment. "It will be okay. I'll get to a place where I can call for help."

"I…" Margot's eyes were wide. "I'm afraid to lose you."

An emotion stronger than fear poured through Heather. "It will be okay," she repeated, tears threatening to choke off the words. "Take Tina and go now. I'll get help and find you again. Try to stay out of sight."

Without giving herself any more time to think about it, Heather turned and ran back in the direction of the car.

SEVENTEEN

Bill and Egan didn't speak much as they drove across the dusty acres that surrounded the lab. Tank stood in the back, his ears and jowls flapping in the wind. Bill's stomach tightened with anticipation. This time he would be one step ahead of Oscar.

He thought about calling Rudley, but decided against it. Until he had confirmation that Oscar was indeed holed up at the abandoned construction site, there was no point in alerting anyone. In another ten miles he'd know for sure.

Egan sat tense in the passenger seat, clutching the seat belt with one hand.

Bill felt slightly sorry for him. The scientist was out of his element. "I can drop you somewhere."

Egan shook his head, licking his dry lips. "No, I'm in this all the way now." He shot Bill a rueful smile. "I never would have guessed I'd be involved in this sort of thing. Excitement is usually something that happens to other people."

Bill nodded, thinking he would personally relish a long stretch with no excitement whatsoever. Maybe after he brought Oscar down.

Maybe. But what would be left for him then?

He'd return to the solitary life he'd built. Just him and Tank and miles of sunbaked land. Maybe he'd tackle the appetizer section of his cookbook. Picturing the cookbook lying open there waiting for him, a wave of melancholy hit him and he knew he did not want to go back to that empty house alone.

He wanted Heather with him.

But it could not be. He could not entertain notions of her while thoughts of vengeance sizzled through his mind. He would not give himself permission to love her or anyone else. How could he make sense of the two opposing forces clashing inside him? His tenderness for Heather in spite of their past, his intense rage at the killer who might be in his grasp momentarily. Confusion filled his mind and he knew he needed to get a handle on it.

Confusion would allow Oscar to escape, and get Bill killed in the process.

God, he thought, *if You're listening, help me sort this all out.*

He felt Egan looking at him. "Do you have any kids, Mr. Cloudman?"

"No. Just two nieces, my sister's girls. You said you have a daughter?"

"Yes." His eyes traveled along the erratic clumps of sod clinging here and there to the side of the road.

"She interested in science like you are?"

He gave a rueful laugh. "No one is interested in old bits of long-ago history. It's only the rare find, the once-in-a-lifetime discovery that gets any attention at all."

And that's been a disappointment to you, Bill thought, reading the sadness in Egan's face.

Egan pushed his glasses up. "I got into geology because it was more practical than paleontology, but at the core, I just want to be out there." He swept a hand over the twisted miles of parched land speckled with the occasional clump of tufted grass burned a fiery hue by the setting sun. "Looking for the secrets waiting for me. It's ironic that I work in a state-of-the-art facility, a place people would give their right arms to see, but I really just want to be outside poking around in the dirt." He sighed. "I admired Leanne, you know."

Bill started. "Admired her?"

"Yes. She had the freedom to explore and she knew this area so well. I asked her to show me around all the corners of this town, but I'm afraid we never got the chance." He looked suddenly stricken. "I'm sorry. I shouldn't be bringing up your sister. I'm sure it hurts you."

Bill shrugged. "It does. But it's good to talk about her, too."

"What I can't figure out is why Oscar Birch would want to kill her. Do you think she came upon him doing something illegal?"

As the sun sank into the horizon, the sky changed from orange to purple. "I don't know. But when I catch him, I'm going to find out."

Egan pointed suddenly. "There. You see that warehouse? It's nearly hidden by the rise of that hill."

Bill took out his binoculars and scanned the area. It was indeed an old warehouse, closed tight. Parked around the entrance were various types of heavy machinery, from backhoes to front loaders. He looked carefully for any signs of movement, but saw none. He got out and peered at the dry grasses that covered the area and the gravel road that served as an entrance to the spot.

He got back into the car. "I'm going to take you back to town now."

Egan blinked. "Has Oscar been here? Did I guess correctly?"

"*Someone* has been coming and going recently. The gravel's compressed. I'm going to get you out of here and come back to stake it out for a while."

"Should I call the police? Have them send backup?"

Bill guided the truck down the road. "No. I'll call in if I get any visual confirmation."

"What should I do then?"

He looked so eager to help, Bill almost smiled. "You've done enough just showing me the place."

Egan smiled. "Not quite like discovering the next La Brea Tar Pits, but I guess I'll have to settle for finding some old construction equipment."

Bill's eyes narrowed. "If this pans out, you've found a lot more than that."

After he delivered Egan safely back, Bill returned to the abandoned warehouse and pulled the truck behind a screen of trees that provided both shade and cover. He settled in to wait as the clock ticked its way to seven.

It was still hot. Tank had gotten out of the truck and parked himself in the shelter of a few scrubby bushes after drinking some water that Bill provided. There was only heat and silence, broken by an occasional flutter of a red-winged blackbird in the cottonwood tree, searching for the last meal of the day.

Left alone with his thoughts, he remembered Leanne. Egan was right. She did have the freedom to explore and she enjoyed it, bringing home pretty rocks and gem fragments she collected on the way. She had a glass jar of them that still sat on his desk. He could imagine her smile as she held up some pebble or shard as if it was a priceless treasure.

He would give anything to see that smile one more time.

Helplessness grated at him.

Oscar would go to prison for murdering her and Johnny and Hazel. It was the only thing he could do for any of them now. But what was to be done about the other matter? The one that pierced him deep inside. He'd been so ready to believe that she was using again, he'd accepted the cause of death instead of questioning it. The shame squeezed at his heart. His lack of trust in his sister was unforgivable. Did it bleed over into his feelings for Heather?

Deep down was he afraid to trust that Heather had made herself a new life? That she was a different person, stronger than she'd ever been before he'd arrested her? Or was he afraid to believe that she still had feelings for him, because it would make him vulnerable all over again?

You let two people down, Bill, two people who counted on you. Leanne and Johnny are gone forever and it's your fault.

Memories of his sister came unexpectedly, her laughter, her good-natured smile, the warmth that drew people to her. A strange feeling sparked in his chest. It was as if a cool breeze had blown gently through his soul. He knew the truth in that moment—that Leanne would have forgiven him. For that matter, he believed Johnny would have, too.

It startled him.

Why? Why did he believe that the two people he'd let down would forgive him?

Where would that forgiveness come from, when life had been so blatantly unfair to both of them?

His breath caught.

From God.

It played in his mind like the remembered lyrics of a song he used to know.

People could forgive each other because they'd been shown how by God, when He sent His son to die for them.

For Leanne.

For Johnny.

For Bill Cloudman.

He felt like a child who had been shown a great treasure, like Egan's elusive big find.

God was still there, after so much anger and rage and loss.

God was still there for Bill.

And He still offered forgiveness for those who asked.

In the sultry quiet of that moment, Bill bowed his head and did just that.

The sweetness rolled around in his heart and healed something there. He remembered that he was loved by God in spite of every mistake he'd ever made. He was forgiven and, what was more, he'd remembered how to forgive.

Looking at the almost full moon that blinked to life in the sky, he hoped he'd have the chance to tell Heather about it.

Heather stopped next to a prickle bush and listened. At first she could hear only the sound of her breath rasping loud in the still air. Shadows all around seemed to close in, leaving her disoriented. Forcing her body to calm itself, she listened again. The sound of footsteps on the road came floating down from above. Heavy booted feet, cautious steps. It must be Oscar. For the moment he was heading away from them.

She wouldn't have long before he figured out which way Tina and Margot were headed. She slid out her cell phone. Still no signal. Fighting a rising panic, Heather began to climb as quickly as she could back up the steep bank. There was a radio in the car. All she'd need was a minute at the most to call for help.

The slope was peppered with loose gravel and in the growing darkness she grabbed at a nearby stone. It gave way in her hands, and she fell heavily. Something wriggled out from the spot where the stone had been.

Heather barely managed to control her scream as a snake reared its head, spread its neck and hissed angrily. She lay on her stomach, face-to-face with the angry monster, its three-foot body coiled for striking.

She felt the hair on the back of her neck rise as the white fangs caught the dying sunlight. Fear scared all practical thoughts from her mind. The only thing she could focus on was those razor-sharp fangs and the shrill hiss of the angry reptile.

Then Bill's words came back to her from one of their many hiking adventures. *It's a hognose snake—they're great actors.*

Sweat beaded on her face as she reached a hand around in the dirt for something to scare the snake.

The reptile continued to hiss, body taut and menacing. Her fingers closed over a stick. Gripping it as tightly as she could in her clammy fingers, she brought it up quickly and slapped it down in the direction of the snake. It didn't make contact—at least she didn't think it had—but the snake rolled over with a gasp and lay still.

They protect themselves by playing dead, Bill had said.

She scooted away as far as she could from the snake before getting back on her feet and continuing her climb toward the highway. The skin on her hands was rubbed raw from scrambling for a hold, fingernails broken and torn. Just before she reached the road, she stopped and listened again.

A scratching noise made her freeze. After a second or two she saw the flame of a match spring to life, and the glowing end of a cigarette shone through the darkness. Oscar was about six feet to her right, standing on the side of the road, looking in the direction that Margot and Tina had taken.

He paused there, the glow of his cigarette waxing and waning as he puffed. Which way would he go? And what would she do if he decided to stand and wait? She didn't think it was likely, since the car was still stopped in the middle of the road. Oscar must have come to the same conclusion, because he coughed slightly and turned on his heel, heading toward Margot and Tina.

Heather's blood ran cold in spite of the heat. With Margot's weakened leg and Tina probably near panic, he would find them quickly. She looked around frantically for something, anything to keep Oscar away. A round rock about the size of a small orange caught her eye. Quickly she hefted it in her hands. Oscar had his back to her now. It would be nearly impossible to throw it with enough force to knock him out. Distraction was the best she could hope for. Aiming across the road, she hurled the rock as far back into the shrubbery as she could before ducking back down.

She heard Oscar stop.

Her heart felt as if it would explode at any minute.

Then came the sound of feet moving across the road toward the spot where she'd thrown the rock.

Faint with relief, she took a moment to gather enough strength in her legs to move. After a quick look to be sure Oscar had walked past the bend in the road, Heather scrambled the rest of the way up the slope and ran toward the car, quickly circling around to the driver's door.

Rudley was slumped over the steering wheel. As quietly as she could she eased open the car door and pulled him back. Blood covered his head and stained the collar of his shirt. Forcing herself to press her fingers to his sticky neck, she found a pulse.

"Thank You, God," she whispered. Leaning across Rudley, she grabbed the radio, fingers cold with terror as she pressed the buttons. There was no comforting buzz of static or glow of lights, so she pressed it harder.

Work, radio. Work.

It was then that she noticed the severed cord. Oscar had taken care of every detail.

Almost crying with frustration, she tried her own cell again with no better result.

She sank down, panting.

Think of something, her nerves screamed. Oscar would

realize soon enough that he'd been tricked. She had to have protection. A weapon.

Rudley had a gun.

Heather reached around him and fumbled for the holster. It took some tugging before she finally freed it, checking quickly to be sure it was loaded before she stuck it behind her back in the waistband of her jeans.

Her plan to summon help had died. Straining her ears for any sign that Oscar was returning, she heard none. The only option was to get to Margot and Tina ahead of him and find someplace better to hide.

She was about to run back toward the creek when a thought occurred to her. Rudley must have a phone, a satellite phone that would get a signal even here in this place sandwiched between the cliffs.

Patting his pockets quickly, she came up with nothing until she felt a phone clipped to his belt. With a surge of triumph she snatched it.

EIGHTEEN

When he decided it was dark enough to provide some cover, Bill got out and quietly called to Tank. They set off across the flat acres of dry grass, which afforded them few places to hide. He took a zigzag route in case Oscar was already waiting, ready to shoot, which he didn't expect. But then, he'd been wrong about plenty of things where Oscar was concerned. When he reached the building, he plastered himself against the side, listening. Tank stood quietly, watching Bill's face for any sign that he should go into attack mode. Bill drew comfort from Tank's presence. The dog would take on anyone to protect his master.

It might just require the both of us to bring down Oscar Birch.

The metal structure was hot to the touch, the corrugated walls burning into his back where he leaned. He listened for a while longer before making his way swiftly to the back door. The handle was fastened shut with a sturdy chain and padlock. Bill stopped. Maybe he'd been wrong again.

He ducked closer, shining a penlight on the padlock to find that it was not clicked completely shut, nor was it rigged to explode. A feeling of satisfaction swelled inside him. Now he had some reason to believe that Oscar really had been using the place for a hideout. Still, he couldn't pull Rudley or any

Tribal Rangers off their other duties until he had proof. Especially since they were now down a man.

The thought made him grimace. If he could ever have used Al Crow by his side, now was that time. But Al had messed up in a huge way. He remembered the look of shame on Crow's face at his error in judgment. Could Bill ever trust him again?

He refocused. *Get your head in the game, Bill, or Oscar wins. It's that simple.*

He removed the padlock and unwound the chain as quietly as he could. The door eased open with a creak. Bill put a finger to his lips as Tank watched. He knew the dog understood and would be as stealthy as a hundred-pound rottweiler could be. They entered the stifling space.

The smell of oil and rust tickled his nose as his eyes adjusted to the gloom. At least a half dozen pieces of construction equipment were parked inside, like some museum of heavy-lifting machines. Each wall of the long rectangular building housed six levels of shelves packed with neatly labeled boxes. Bill appreciated the tidiness even as he noted all the possible hiding places. His only advantage was Tank. Oscar could hide from Bill, but not from a determined canine.

Gun in hand, he began to ease along the perimeter of the warehouse, checking each shelf for gaps big enough for a man to tuck himself into. Tank stiffened and raced to the last shelving unit. Bill followed, muscles tight, breath caught in his lungs. The dog plunged into an empty space on the bottom shelf.

Bill jerked around, gun pointed at the opening. Tank was deep into the gap with only his hind end sticking out. It was not Oscar, Bill knew that much. The guy was small, but not small enough to pack himself into that spot. Lowering his weapon, he called softly to the dog. Tank backed out of the space.

Peering into the hole, Bill saw nothing. Had the dog caught a lingering scent of some rodent or snake?

He didn't take the time to consider it further as they continued their slow check of the building. This time when Tank went on alert, it was next to a dirt-spattered front loader. With a small whine, Tank sniffed deeply at the front scoop and each tire. Bill did a quick check under the vehicle, but saw nothing.

He was about to move on, but Tank remained focused on the vehicle, pawing at the enormous tires, rising on his hind legs to reach the glassed-in driver's compartment. There was no visible sign of anyone up there, but Bill knew enough to trust the dog.

He readied his gun again and climbed up onto the monstrous tire. Grasping the handle, he took a calming breath and jerked the door open.

There was no sound except the dog's paws scrabbling on metal as he launched himself up into the driver's seat, turning in excited circles.

Bill saw the reason for Tank's excitement. Inside was a neat stack of clothes, including a folded mail carrier's uniform. Next to it were several bottles of water, a can of salted peanuts, a packet of beef jerky, a laptop and a small generator.

He knew Oscar wasn't here at the moment, but he didn't care. The man was going to be back and Bill was going to be ready. He patted Tank. "Good boy."

They climbed down and Bill made his way back to the truck, excitement welling inside him.

Stay calm, he warned himself. *This time you've got to take him down for good.*

He didn't want to involve the police, but he knew it would

be both selfish and stupid to attempt the apprehension himself. He wasn't a police officer anymore and, as much as he longed for the chance to avenge Johnny and Leanne, it had to be done by the book. He had freed his phone, when it vibrated in his hand.

Surprised, he answered.

"Hello, Billy." Aunt Jean's voice sounded loud and out of place.

He had to keep the conversation short. "I'm in the middle of something right now, but I'll call you back soon. How is Tina getting along?"

"That's what I'm calling about."

He bit back a sigh. Of course the little girl would be having problems after watching her uncle collapse. "What's wrong?"

"She isn't here, that's what's wrong."

Bill jerked. "Did she run away again?"

"No, honey. She never came. I've been expecting that Rudley fellow to drive up any minute, but so far no sign of him. He didn't specify an exact time he'd be here, but I cooked a nice supper for them."

Bill's stomach dropped as he checked his watch. It was seven-thirty. He'd watched Rudley pull out of Charlie's driveway two hours ago. "They should have been there by now."

"That's what I thought. Do you suppose they stopped for dinner or something?"

He tried to keep his tone calm. "I'll make some calls and get back to you."

"Bill?" There was a quiver in her voice. "Should I be worried?"

He wanted to tell her no, that Rudley had stopped somewhere to treat Tina to ice cream or something. Maybe they'd gotten a flat tire or had engine trouble. But he knew deep down it was none of the above. Rudley knew the stakes. He wouldn't have stopped anywhere for long. "I'll call you soon," he said, disconnecting quickly before she could ask anything else.

He dialed Rudley's cell. It rang and went to voice mail.

The second call went to the Tribal Ranger office.

"No, Agent Rudley hasn't reported in," he was told.

"Something's wrong. He didn't arrive at my aunt's house. Check into it."

If the dispatcher hadn't known him, she might have dismissed his commands, but he knew her, the same woman, ironically, who had dispatched an ambulance after Johnny was killed. "I will right now," she said.

There was nothing he could do by tearing out of here. Oscar would expect him to follow as soon as he got word that something was wrong. It was what Oscar would expect, perhaps what he'd planned on, and Bill would probably walk right into an ambush.

But he was not about to let Oscar harm Heather or Tina in any way, or Margot, either, for that matter. Trap or no trap, he would go.

God, I know I haven't been in communication with You for a while, but I'm here now.

And I need help.

As she stood by the car, wishing there was something she could do for Rudley, the phone vibrated in Heather's hand. It startled her so much she dropped it and it skidded underneath the crumpled vehicle. She was down on her hands and knees trying to fish it out when she heard Oscar return, feet scuffing along the gravel, the faint scent of cigarette smoke getting stronger. Her breath froze. Gooseflesh erupted all over her skin. She scurried around to the other side of the car, the side that looked down onto the dry gully below.

She heard rather than saw Oscar take out his own phone.

"Yes?" he said softly.

After a moment of silence he sighed. "Thank you for letting me know. Things are just fine here."

Fine? The man truly was sick. Who would he be talking to?

She strained to listen, but there was no further conversation. Oscar must have pocketed his phone again. She smelled the acrid smoke from his cigarette as her stomach roiled with indecision. Should she try to locate the phone? Risking a quick peek under the car, she could not see anything in the darkness. Rooting around underneath would make enough noise to attract his attention.

She might ease away from the car, scoot back down the slope and try to make it to Tina and Margot. But how would that improve things? Without the phone, she still had no way to summon help and her movements would probably alert him.

She could think of only one other choice. To creep away from the car in the direction they had been driving, to lure Oscar as far from her mother and Tina as she could. She listened again, risking a quick look around the back tire.

He stood there, as still as if he were carved from moonlit stone, the glowing tip of the cigarette flickering in the near darkness. After one more unsuccessful look under the car, she eased back on her hands and knees, crawling inch by inch. Bits of rock cut into her palms as she placed them slowly and painfully.

Did no one else ever use this road? she thought in exasperation. There was no sign of any other vehicle that might stop and help.

At least Rudley was alive.

If Oscar let him stay that way.

The thought added a new layer of horror to the situation.

Closer and closer she crept to the nearest tree, a scraggly, twisted thing she could not even identify in the gloom. At the moment, it was her greatest friend. If she could get to that shelter without being spotted, she might have the tiniest chance of making a break for it. A few miles down the road and she could start to make some noise, to draw Oscar in the direction she wanted him to go.

The tree was only two feet away now, but the shoulder narrowed to a scant six inches. She squeezed along, knowing that if she toppled down the slope it was all over. One more foot and the tree was within touching distance. She reached out a hand as if she could somehow bring it closer just by sheer force of will.

"Do you know the time?"

Heather froze, unable to even look up.

Oscar had moved around the edge of the car. "I guess maybe you don't have your watch with you. Of course, there's the phone." He laughed. "But that's underneath the car, isn't it? Pity you didn't get to it. It might have saved you quite a lot of work."

Terror rippling through her body, she got to her feet to face him.

The white of his bald scalp shone in the moonlight. And that terrible grin.

She could think of nothing to say as she stared at him.

"That was clever to try to misdirect me. I can see why Bill enjoys your company. You are strong, stronger than he is, most likely."

"You want me," she managed. "So here I am."

"True enough. There you are. Go get Rudley's phone out from underneath the car, will you?"

She was stunned. He would allow her to have the phone? Of course not. He'd take it and finish her off. Then she remembered the gun tucked in the back of her pants. If she could have a moment, just one second out of his sight.

"Okay." Dropping back to her knees, she eased as flat as she could, feeling Oscar's eyes on her every move. Pushing herself down and blinking against the grit that found its way into her eyes, she patted her hands around in a show of finding the phone. It was there, all right, tucked against the rear wheel. She gripped it in one hand and made sure the gun was easily accessible with the other. When she handed over the phone she'd have only a moment.

The thought of pulling the trigger made her go cold inside, but it was the only way she could save Rudley, her mother and Tina.

And Bill.

In that moment, she wished more than anything that she could feel the warmth of Bill's embrace one more time, to relive the rare moments of laughter they'd shared. She did not know if God would ever give her the chance even to say goodbye to Bill before he returned to his life of solitude and she to her career, but it didn't stop the longing from rising in a powerful tide inside her.

God, help me.

The lives of five people rode on the next sixty seconds.

Heather slid out from underneath the car, ignoring the dirt that made its way up her pant legs as she did so. Climbing to her feet, she moved closer and saw Oscar standing with his hand outstretched, ready to take the phone. In the other, he cupped some object she could not make out in the dim light. He was now standing at the extreme edge of the road, where it dropped off into the ravine below.

She handed it to him, fingers trembling.

He reached out a calloused hand to take it.

She whipped the gun from her waistband and pointed it at him.

His eyes widened. "Well, well. You *are* a resourceful one. Rudley's gun, I assume?"

Heather ignored him. "Here's what you're going to do. You're going to lie down on the ground and I'm going to call for help. If you move, I'll shoot you."

He raised an eyebrow. "I've been told you know how to handle a gun. Very impressive, but that's not what's going to happen."

It was a trick to unsettle her and she ignored it. "Lie down on the ground right now."

He laughed, a grating, unnatural noise. "While I appreciate your bravado, there's something you should see. Down there."

He jerked his head at the dry riverbed below.

Heather figured it must be a trick and didn't move.

"I'm afraid I didn't really fall for your distraction technique," Oscar continued. "It wasn't hard for me to circle around and find them."

She felt a chill creep into her body. "What did you do?"

"Nothing, just secured them in place for the time being. There." He cocked his head down below. "At the bottom."

Feeling the panic inside beginning to mount, Heather took a few steps toward the edge, keeping a keen eye on Oscar. He made no attempt to move. Risking a quick peek, she saw them, her mother and Tina, hands tied together around the base of a tree, mouths covered with some sort of tape.

She gripped the gun. "Fine. Then I'll have to shoot you and go and get them."

"You could," he said, holding out his cupped hand. "But I wouldn't recommend it. Do you see what I've got here, Heather?" His tone grew harsh.

The rising moon shone on the object in his hand, and she knew in that moment she'd lost.

"It's a pineapple grenade. Not used too much anymore, but they sure served their purpose in World War II and Vietnam. As you can see, I've already pulled the safety ring, so if you shoot me, I'll drop it, of course. It will roll down the slope here and detonate at the bottom." He held his arm over the side.

Heather's vision swam. What was she supposed to do? Her palms grew clammy and the gun trembled in her hands.

"Make your decision, Heather. I'm not as young as I used to be and my arm's getting a little shaky."

"You wouldn't do it."

He stared. "Why not? I don't care a lick about your mother or that girl. Or you, for that matter. You're bait, nothing more, and you'll do the job just fine alone." A fleck of spittle flew out of his mouth. "I don't care if they live or die."

The words echoed around her mind. He was telling the truth. He would not hesitate to drop the grenade and kill them just as easily as he'd shot Agent Rudley.

With a sick feeling of dread, she lowered the gun and let it fall to the ground. "I will do anything you tell me, if you don't hurt them."

His smile was luminous in the dark. "I know."

NINETEEN

Bill called to Tank and started the engine. Idling there, he called Rudley's number one more time, startled when Heather answered.

"Bill?"

His body shuddered in relief. "Where are you?" he managed.

"I'm…"

There was the sound of the phone changing hands. "Hello, Bill."

Bill felt the bottom fall out of his stomach. His worst fear since the moment he'd learned Oscar was on the loose again had come true.

Oscar had Heather.

"Don't hurt her."

"Don't hurt her? Like you didn't hurt my son, Bill?" Oscar's voice simmered with rage.

As much as Bill wanted to lash out, he knew he had to play along, to find out where they were.

"We both know you want me. Tell me where you are and I'll be there. The girl isn't important."

"Oh, I think she is. And I'm going to tell you what's going to happen next because I'm in charge here. Do you understand that, Bill?"

"Yes. I understand."

"This will be easy. You're already at the construction site."

Bill jerked in surprise. How did he know that?

"Are you still there, Bill?"

"Yes."

"Good. Then all you have to do is be a good boy and stay there. We should be along shortly."

Bill's mind raced. "Where's Agent Rudley? And the others?"

"That's all you need to know right now, except for one more thing."

"Tell me."

"You won't summon any cops or Tribal Rangers. No law enforcement of any kind. There's only one road in and out. If I see one sign that anyone else is waiting there but you, I will kill these girls, one at a time. Do you understand me?"

Bill forced the words over his dry tongue. "I understand. Just me, and you won't hurt them."

Oscar laughed. "See you soon, Bill."

He stared at the phone. This had to be a nightmare. How could this man have complete power over him?

Because he had Tina.

And Heather's mother.

And Heather.

If he hurt Heather, took her away forever… Bill could not stand to think it.

His mind raced. If Oscar was monitoring the property somehow, he would easily spot any police or FBI cars, and Bill knew the threats to kill the women were not idle ones. Oscar cared little for people outside his family.

Frustration clawed at his mind. He got out of the car to pace, Tank right along with him. Oscar had all the bargaining chips and Bill had no one to call on for help.

A thought struck him. There was one person who could assist, but he'd already made a mistake that left him untrustworthy in Bill's eyes. He'd lost everything and Bill figured he probably deserved it.

Deserved it.

Bill let the thought linger in his mind before another took its place.

And he deserved forgiveness, too.

Bill dialed the phone.

After a brief conversation, he settled in to wait. Unable to stand the stillness, he paced up and down the long gravel drive, checking and rechecking his gun and the extra rounds, looking for the slightest indication that Oscar was getting closer. The time ticked away in slow-motion minutes. Eight-thirty. Eight forty-five. It was almost nine by the time he saw Al. As it was, the man was a scant fifty feet away before Bill knew he was there and only then because Tank went on alert.

"Easy there," Al said, giving Tank a pat.

Bill realized he had drawn his weapon. He holstered it and they stood near the cover of the shrubs. "I didn't hear your horse."

"That's the idea. I stayed off the roads, stuck to the trails. Status?"

"No sign of him yet. Any word?"

"Guy out hunting found Rudley. They transported him to County. He's alive. No one else found on the scene. You sure you don't want to bring them in on this?"

Bill shook his head. "Oscar meant what he said. He'll kill them if he spots cops."

"That why you called me?" The regret shone on Al's face, even in the moonlight. "I'm not really a cop anymore?"

Bill sighed. "No, Al. I called you because you have been my friend for twenty years. You screwed up, yeah, but so have I. If I'm ever going to be forgiven for my heap of mess-ups, then I guess I can see my way clear to forgiving one of yours."

Al's voice broke. "Thanks."

"You're not going to thank me later. Oscar is out for my blood, but he won't hesitate to kill you, too. You sure you want to be here?"

Al nodded, eyes glittering. "Nowhere else I'd rather be."

They talked out a plan and Al disappeared into the darkness.

In spite of what was about to come, Bill felt that some corner of his soul was at peace. At least he could go to his death knowing that.

The luminous hands of his watch crept along and still no sign of Oscar.

He resisted the urge to kick at the tires of his truck.

Where were they?

Heather's ears still rang with the sound of Bill's voice before Oscar had snatched away the phone. Oscar looked as if he had thoroughly enjoyed the conversation. And why not? He had Bill right where he wanted him, squirming, and deeply afraid.

How unfair it was that love could make you so terribly vulnerable. She startled herself with the thought. Bill still cared about her on some level, she knew, enjoyed the memories of the sweet love they'd shared, but her feelings for him had rekindled the moment she had seen him and it was more than fond memories of the past. She loved him, desperately, and that love would stay one-sided, she was just as sure. Watching Oscar's satisfied smile, she believed none of them would be alive very long to worry about it, unless she figured out some way to escape and contact Bill.

Oscar slid the phone into his pocket and whistled cheerfully, the grenade still in his hand. Then he locked eyes on hers.

His face morphed into an expression of pure evil as he tossed the grenade down the slope toward Margot and Tina.

"No!" Heather screamed, running to the side until Oscar caught her by the hair.

"Stay here with me, and listen for the bang," he hissed in her ear.

Struggling with Oscar, terror firing her nerves, she could not get away. All she could do was watch in horror as the grenade bounced and rolled, coming to rest at her mother's feet.

Oh, God! she screamed silently. *Don't take her away again.*

The seconds ticked away and she suddenly realized Oscar was laughing. He let go of her abruptly and she went down on one knee.

"It was a dud. You should have seen the look on your face," Oscar said, wiping away tears with the back of his gun hand. "I'll bet you feel good and stupid now for handing over the gun, don't you?"

Rage built up inside and she would have struck at him if he hadn't pointed the weapon at her.

"Now, go down there and get them. Bring them back up. If you try anything I'll kill the kid first, then your mother. Move it."

On rubbery legs Heather slipped and slid her way down the slope, all the while trying to figure out a plan for escape. She still had her own phone, but there most likely was no signal, and if she took it out of her pocket, Oscar would see it light up.

The scraggly tree to which her mother and Tina were tied offered little cover and they would be exposed for several yards before they could find something else to hide behind.

Think, Heather, think. She berated herself as she closed the gap between them. Why hadn't she insisted on sending her mother away from South Dakota? Why?

The answer, true as it was, did not help matters.

She loved her mother. In spite of the abandonment, her complete parental failure, the years of grief, Heather loved her mother. As she drew near, Tina's gaze followed her every move and her mother's eyes filled, a tear trickling down her face and over the tape that covered her mouth.

Through her own tears, Heather began trying to loosen the rope. She remembered her mother's earlier words.

I love you, though I haven't earned the right and you will likely never return that love.

How is that possible?

I think that you would probably say it's because of God, wouldn't you?

She pulled harder at the ropes until her fingernails tore and finally the bonds loosened. Tina peeled the tape off her own mouth and grabbed Heather around the waist. Her mother slid to the ground.

"That bad man..." Tina spluttered, her nose running. "He tied us up. He's bad, bad, bad."

Heather tried to comfort her and check on her mother at the same time. "I know, honey, I know. He is a bad man, but we need to do what he says right now, just for a while."

She knelt on the gravelly soil and pulled the tape as gently as she could away from her mother's mouth. For a moment they stared at each other in silence, hands gripped together.

Margot tried several times before she got the words out. "He's still up there?"

She nodded.

"Were you able to call for help?"

Heather felt an overwhelming sense of failure. "No. We're going to meet Bill."

Margot squeezed her daughter's hand. "You did your best."

But her best was not enough to save them. Why couldn't she think of a way out, some plan that would buy them time at least?

Oscar shouted down from the road. "Get up here."

Tina whimpered again as Heather helped her mother to her feet. Margot reached out a hand, very gently, and stroked Heather's face.

"I am very proud that you are my daughter."

Heather's throat closed up, leaving her unable to answer.

Very proud.

Daughter.

There were no sweeter words, nothing she had longed to hear more in her entire life. And now they'd been given to her just before they were all likely to die.

Margot took Tina around the shoulders. The girl buried her face in Margot's shirt, and Margot stroked Tina's hair before she gave Heather a final look.

"We'll make it as easy for the child as we can," she whispered.

Heather nodded through her tears and they began the trudge back up the slope to the place where Oscar waited.

"Walk that way," he ordered when they had made it back to the road. Holding hands, the three walked as best as they could in the darkness to a spot a few miles down the road, where they found a dusty blue sedan.

"All three in front," he barked, poking Heather with the gun. "You drive."

She was surprised he would allow her to take the wheel, until he got into the backseat and pressed the gun to the back of her neck.

"If you do anything funny, I'll kill the kid first. Then your mother."

She could feel Tina's body go rigid beside her. Risking a quick pat to her knee, she said, "Nothing funny, so you won't need to hurt anyone."

"What time is it?" Oscar asked.

Margot answered, her voice remarkably strong. "Nine."

"All right, then, we've got plenty of time. Drive."

Plenty of time? The realization hit Heather. Plenty of time until midnight, when the day changed. Plenty of time for Oscar to make his murderous deadline. With no other choice, she put the car in Drive and eased out of the shrubs onto the road.

She did not recognize where they were going at first. Close to an hour later it came to her. The lab. They were heading toward the DUSEL. It raised a spark of hope inside her. The place was monitored and secure. Someone would see them, surely, a security guard maybe.

The spark died as they passed the lab, the comforting lights from the building fading into the distance behind them.

"Slow down," Oscar said. "Coming up on it on the left. We're early, but I don't think Bill will mind dying a little ahead of schedule."

She saw nothing but flat grassland until he ordered her to turn on a narrow path that she would have missed. It was more a trail than a road, and the car bumped and jostled over the uneven ground.

They stopped at Oscar's instruction. He dialed the phone. "Bill. Enjoying your evening?"

Heather's heart squeezed. It could not be that they were going to witness Oscar kill Bill. How could she watch helplessly as the man she loved was gunned down? To be followed by her mother and Tina?

There had to be something she could do.

Think, Heather.

"We're here now—your girls, too. I will meet you in front of the warehouse. Lock up your dog and stand with your hands in the air. If I see you go for a gun, or any cops arrive, you know what is going to happen."

He clicked off and pressed the gun into her neck again. She saw her mother tense.

"Drive slowly and remember what the price will be if you get creative."

She drove, the car creeping so slowly it hardly raised any dust. All the while her mind raced.

Bill.

How she had hurt him, not by her drinking but by shutting him out of her life when he wanted to help. Now she was going to watch him die, murdered at the hands of a madman, and he would never know how much she loved him, how very sorry she was for hurting him.

Some part of her mind would not accept it. Surely there were cops waiting, concealed in the warehouse maybe.

The FBI must have realized Agent Rudley had not reported in. Perhaps they'd sent help and even now the place was surrounded.

As they pulled to a stop in front of the warehouse, she knew her ideas were just desperate imaginings.

Bill stepped forward out of the shadows, quite alone, his empty hands held toward the night sky.

TWENTY

As soon as Oscar got out of the car, Tank went crazy, barking and clawing at the window. Bill did not try to quiet him. The dog behaved exactly as Bill would have if he wasn't so afraid for the women in the car. Emotions raced through him as he sought Heather's eyes behind the windshield and saw them rounded in terror, her face pale as milk.

Tina's and Margot's expressions were concealed by shadows and he was grateful. They were alive for the moment and that's all he could ask for.

His heart hammered inside and he felt a bead of sweat slide down his forehead. He needed only a moment, a way to get Oscar off guard for a fraction of a second. Al Crow was concealed somewhere and he prayed Al would find a way to buy him that time.

Oscar stepped out and closed the door behind him, gun leveled at Bill. He ordered Heather out of the car and told her to bring the car keys. She obeyed. Bill wanted to reassure her, to tell her he would get them out of this mess, but he couldn't. He'd never lied to her and he wasn't going to start now.

Oscar positioned Heather close, her back to the driver's door, and retrained the gun on her.

"I've been waiting a long time for this moment, Cloudman."

"Me, too," Bill said, his mind whirling. With Heather so close, Al would be afraid to take a shot for fear of hitting Heather or the two people still in the car. He had to keep Oscar talking and hope for an opening.

Tank's frenzy increased and he slammed at the truck window.

"I didn't expect to have so many extra bodies around, but life is unpredictable and you've got to roll with the punches." Oscar grinned.

"They have nothing to do with it. You want me because I am responsible for Autie's death, isn't that right?"

Heather gasped as the words hit their mark. Oscar stiffened. "Yes, and you will die like the cowardly dog you are, but not until you see them die first. I want to see the suffering on your face."

"First, tell me. Why did you kill my sister?"

He shrugged. "She was too close to finding it." He laughed. "Now that I know she was your sister, I should have found a more painful way for her to die instead of a blow to the head and an injection to make it look like she overdosed. A quick push over the cliff and it was done."

A red mist filled Bill's vision as he struggled for self-control. "She was close to finding what?"

"My chance for the big payoff. My one chance to make sure my son had everything he deserved. I could have made it all happen, but your sister was close to figuring it out. She was nosy, just like you and just like Hazel."

"I still don't understand. What was the payoff?"

Oscar hesitated a moment. "Doesn't matter. You don't get to know all the answers. I do. I know all the secrets and I choose not to let you in on them." Oscar's gloating distracted him from two important details—the faintest squeak of metal from the warehouse roof and the slow movement of Heather's hand as she slid her fingers into her pocket.

It was an innocent gesture and Bill had no idea what she planned, but he caught the look on her face, desperate yet determined. With a Herculean effort he kept his eyes fixed on Oscar. "So I'll die never knowing why you killed my sister."

Oscar laughed. "Exactly."

The next moment unrolled in a frantic haze. Heather pulled something out of her pocket and threw it into Oscar's face. Whatever it was, it caused him to jerk back just as Al Crow dropped down from the roof of the warehouse and Bill lunged at Oscar. There was a shot fired, but Bill didn't have time to track where it went.

They tumbled over and over on the dusty ground, Tank barking viciously until Bill heard the sound of breaking glass and the dog smashed his way out of the truck, grabbing the back of Oscar's jacket between his teeth.

It was all Bill could do to hold on to Oscar, whose fury gave him the strength of a much bigger man. They grappled, Bill desperately trying to keep Oscar's gun from firing in the direction of the women.

Tank continued to savage Oscar's coat.

"I'll kill you," Oscar hissed between grunts.

Bill didn't answer. He was not going to let this man go unless it was to a prison cell. The gun fired again.

"Heather, get down," he shouted.

He wasn't sure if she did as instructed, because Oscar got a hand loose and struck him in the face. The stinging pain made his eyes water and he felt Oscar roll on top of him. Another shot rang out, followed by another sound of breaking glass.

Bill felt the tide turning. He knew if he didn't rally, Oscar would win.

All he could think of was Heather's chocolate eyes on him, trusting him, loving him. With a muttered prayer and a savage effort he wrenched Oscar's arm to the side. The impact of Oscar's hand striking the car caused the gun to come loose and skitter across the ground. He forced Oscar onto his back and knelt on top of his shoulders, pinning him.

A surge of triumph powered through him and he wiped the sweat from his face. Panting heavily he looked up, stomach dropping when he saw Heather kneeling on the ground.

As soon as she'd seen Al Crow jerk backward after he dropped down from the roof, she knew he'd been shot. Mind a whirl of terror, she shouted to her mother to keep Tina down and ran to the stricken man. While she desperately tried to find the source of his injury, her mind was on Bill. Did Al have a gun that she could use to help fend off Oscar?

Al groaned and Heather was reassured. He was alive at least. Where was his gun? It must have come loose in his fall. Patting him along the sides, she felt the armored vest under his shirt. Kevlar. She exhaled, keeping one eye on Bill as he struggled with Oscar.

She saw the hole where the bullet had entered near his ribs, but it had not penetrated the Kevlar. She sighed in relief as he began to stir, her heart leaping when she saw his rifle a few feet away in the bushes.

Bill was yelling something and she saw with a surge of dizzying relief that he seemed to have gotten Oscar under control. His stricken face told her his thoughts.

"Al's okay," she yelled. Then she found a pair of elastic restraints in Al's pockets and tossed them to Bill before she grabbed the rifle.

Bill managed to get Tank off long enough to tie Oscar's hands. Then he stood slowly and peered into the car.

Heather kept the rifle trained on Oscar as her breath caught. Her mother and Tina. Had they been hit? Visions of what Bill might find in the car made her tremble. She started toward the car, her whole body shuddering in terror.

Then the door opened and Margot and Tina got out.

Heather nearly cried at the sight of them, Tina clutched tightly in Margot's arms.

Thank You, God.

Thank You.

Al was trying to stand and she gave him an arm to help. He cursed and moaned as he got to his feet, blinking the grit from his eyes. "Did we get him?"

Heather wanted to shout the news. "Yes. We got him."

Al nodded and took the rifle out of her hands. "I'll cover him."

She handed the weapon over and ran to Bill.

He folded her in his arms and whispered words she could not make out.

It didn't matter. He was safe and it was over.

His arms were tight around her and the thud of his heart on her cheek was the sweetest thing she'd ever felt.

"Are you hurt? Did he hurt you?" Bill whispered.

"No," she said, pulling away to look in his face. "I'm okay. And you got him, Bill. You brought down Oscar Birch."

His voice broke once as he answered, "I had help. What did you toss in his face?"

She fished a tiny object out of her pocket. "Tina's pink beads."

He laughed then, a sound she had not heard in a long time.

They turned to find Al pulling Oscar to his feet as flashing lights began to make their way onto the property, accompanied by the wail of sirens.

Margot waved a handheld radio. "I found the portable radio stuck under the seat. Tina and I called for help."

The look Oscar gave them was pure malice.

"It's a long way to prison, Cloudman. This isn't finished."

"You're right," Bill said. "It won't be finished until you're tried for my sister's murder and the abduction of these three women."

"Not to mention trying to kill off the two of us," Al said, sweat trickling down his face. "I think he should get a nice hefty sentence for that."

Oscar didn't answer and Heather was glad when Al turned him away to greet the arriving police cars.

She noticed Tina was watching Oscar, fingers jammed in her mouth.

The child shouldn't witness the hatred written all over Oscar's face. She went to Tina and turned her away, calling Tank over to distract the girl.

Tank finally left his watch over Oscar and approached Tina for a wet lick to her face.

Heather laughed.

A sound exploded through the air.

She caught a glimpse of Oscar crumpling to the ground, a dark spot visible on his forehead. Then everything was a blur. Officers shouted and took cover. Bill and Al pushed the women toward the shelter of the car and shoved them inside.

"What is it?" she gasped at Bill. "What's happening?"

Bill pressed his body over hers on the backseat while Al did the same to Tina and Margot in the front.

"Somebody just shot Oscar Birch."

"Wh-who…?" she stammered.

His arms tightened on her shoulders and he spoke quietly into her ear. "I don't know. Stay in the car until the scene is secured. We'll get you out of here as soon as we can."

"Bill—" She grabbed at his hand as he pulled away. "What does this mean? I thought it was over."

He cupped her cheek, warm fingers stroking her tearstained face. "I did, too." He moved closer, until his face was so close to hers her breath grew short. He traced his lips along her cheekbones. "At least you're okay. That's all I need to know right now."

He pressed a kiss to the spot where her pulse hammered in her temple. Nerves sparked inside, arcing through her like a jolt of electric current. More than anything, she wanted him to stay here, with her.

"I wanted to tell you…" he whispered.

A Tribal Ranger rapped on the door. Bill got out.

"Shot came from up there," the Ranger said, pointing to a crest of rock fifty yards away. "We saw a motorbike take off, so I think the shooter's gone, but we'll cover the grounds, see what we can find."

Bill nodded. "I want these women taken to safety. Tina needs to stay with them until we know what happened."

He nodded. "Feds are on their way, but we've only got a half dozen guys here right now." He shot a slightly hesitant look at Crow. "Can you drive them back? You can take my car."

Crow nodded. "Okay. Get my horse back, would ya? He's tied under those trees."

Heather didn't want to go anywhere, but she didn't seem to have any choice in the matter. Al instructed them to stay low as he drove the car as quickly as he dared off the property. Try as she might, she could make no sense of what had just happened. For a moment it had been over, Oscar in custody and everyone safe. Then the shot had come out of nowhere, and clearly Oscar was the target.

The memory of Bill's embrace clung to her mind. There was something different about him, but she hadn't had the time to examine things closely.

"Al? How did you happen to be there with Bill?"

"He called me. There was no way to get a car in or out without Oscar knowing, so I rode my horse."

"He called you?" After seeing the rage on Bill's face when he'd found out about Al's failure, she didn't think it was possible.

Al caught her eye in the rearview mirror. "Yeah, surprised me, too. He said if he was ever gonna be forgiven for his mess-ups, he'd better start extending the favor."

Forgiveness? Was Bill finally going to be able to forgive himself for Johnny's death? And would he ever be able to forgive her for her colossal failure? There was no way of knowing until she had a chance to talk to him. What she did know was that in his arms she'd found the happiness that her heart had sought for so long.

After what seemed like an eternity they arrived back at her cabin. It was late, but Heather knew she would not sleep. Not with Bill still out there and some new threat on the loose. Choo Choo greeted them with a wagging tail and slobbery licks. The old dog brought a smile to Tina's face.

Al left to check the property when a federal agent arrived. Heather suspected it had more to do with Al's shame at being relieved of duty than anything else. Margot took Tina to the back room with Choo Choo while Heather met with the agent.

"How's Rudley?" she asked before he had a chance to start the questions.

"Holding his own. Lost a lot of blood, but the bullet didn't hit anything vital."

She sagged in relief. The grief she felt at leaving him there alone and bleeding eased a bit. The agent ran her through the events of the evening down to the last detail.

"Who was Oscar speaking to on the phone after the crash?"

Heather shook her head. "I don't know."

"Was it a male or female voice?"

She knew if she could help figure out who the caller was, it might tell them who killed Oscar. "I'm sorry, I just don't know."

She could see the disappointment on his face before he asked her to fetch her mother for her side of the story. Heather found them in the back bedroom, watching a cartoon on the small TV.

"I don't have any idea what this ridiculous show is about, but it calmed her down," Margot whispered as she returned with Heather to meet the agent.

What followed was another half hour of questioning, with the same result. Margot was no more help in solving the mystery than Heather had been. The agent finally excused himself and went to his car to make phone calls.

They found Tina asleep in front of the television, fingers jammed in her mouth. Heather took off Tina's shoes and they tucked her into the bed. Her face was so small against the pillow, so delicate and innocent. She should never have had to endure what she'd been through that day.

Heather saw in her mother's face that she felt the same way. They tiptoed out of the room. Before they closed the door, Choo Choo heaved himself up onto the bed and curled up next to the girl. Heather gaped. "I didn't know he could even do that."

"I think he knows where he's needed right now," Margot said, turning on the hallway light and leaving the door to the bedroom open. "If she wakes up, she won't be in the dark."

Heather stared at her mother and suddenly everything came crashing in. The kidnapping. Her terror at seeing the grenade rolling down the hill. Tina's scared face. Bill standing unarmed to defy Oscar's hatred. And finally her mother's words when Heather had failed to contact help.

I'm proud of you.

It was too much. Rivers of tears began to flow down Heather's face and she sank to the floor, curled up in a ball, stifling her sobs on the back of her hand. Then she felt the incredible comfort of her mother's arms around her.

TWENTY-ONE

The agent let Bill into Heather's house before sunup. He'd already called Aunt Jean to come and give whatever comfort possible to Tina, and now, as Heather lay on the sofa on her side, face scratched and bruised from the horror of the previous night, he gently stroked her hair. He wished he could be perfectly at ease about the situation, but the fact of the matter was there was still a killer on the loose. It didn't seem as though there was any more direct threat to Heather, but he was never going to forget the sheer terror of knowing she was in the hands of a murderer. Margot appeared in the kitchen and he nodded at her as he moved away.

He wondered how matters stood between Heather and her mother. It was the most important relationship in her life and he knew he needed to stay out of the way while they worked it out, or didn't. That was fine. His own emotions were still a jumble of uncertainty. What should he do now that Oscar was dead? What was his life supposed to be now? It seemed as if something had changed.

"What should I do, God?" he found himself whispering. "Show me."

Margot handed him a cup of coffee and they sat until Heather woke abruptly.

"What?" she gasped.

Bill put a hand over hers. "No news. The gunman, whoever it was, has probably taken off. Could have been a vigilante, or a random shooter."

She blinked. "But you don't think so."

"No. I don't think so. For the moment, though, everything is quiet. That's all I came to tell you."

Was it all? Was he ready to walk out the door again?

Margot raised a hand. "Actually, there's something I wanted to talk to you about, which may be nothing at all."

Bill gave her his attention. "I'm listening."

She pulled a crumpled envelope from her pocket. "These are lab test results from the water samples we took at Mr. Brown's place. I had Agent Rudley stop at the post office on our way—" She shook her head. "Last night."

Heather's mouth fell open. "But Dr. Egan ran the tests at the lab, didn't he?"

"One thing I learned as a scientist is never trust someone else with your data. I took another set of samples and sent them to be analyzed myself. There is evidence of slight uranium contamination in the aquifer. Not high levels, but enough to warrant some attention. The strange thing is that Dr. Egan said the samples were clean, no trace contamination."

Bill frowned, mind turning. "Why would Egan get different results?"

"That was my question precisely."

Bill put the facts together in his mind. "Egan was the one who showed me Oscar's hideout."

"Dr. Egan?" Heather gaped. "You don't think he shot Oscar?"

"I don't know. But it bears looking into. I'll talk to the Feds." Bill took out his phone and dialed, quickly passing along the strange information. He disconnected, facts still whirling in his mind. "Why would Egan want to hide the contamination? Because he didn't want any cleanup teams poking around? What would he need to hide? He doesn't even live in this town."

Heather locked eyes with his. "A cleanup of the aquifer would involve my property and Charlie's. I can't think of much worth hiding in either place."

"But the night I drove you home, there was a trespasser here. Remember? He rode a motorbike. Guys think Oscar's shooter did, too."

Sometimes people get in over their heads and one small choice ensnares them, Egan had said. Had he somehow fallen into an arrangement with Oscar Birch?

"But what in the world is worth killing for here?" Heather murmured.

Margot's face suddenly lit up. "I think I know." She hurried into her room, and returned with the box of Tina's treasures. Quickly she selected a white chunk about two inches long. "I thought it was strange at the time, but with everything that's happened I forgot."

Bill took it from her. "What is it?"

"I have a feeling it's what Dr. Egan will kill for, the big 'payoff' that Oscar talked about. Can you show me the spot where you found the trespasser?"

"I don't think you two should be out in the open until the shooter is caught." He almost laughed at the identical looks of determination on mother and daughter.

"We're going," they both said at once.

Aunt Jean arrived to stay with the still-sleeping Tina. Bill hugged her tight and endured the half dozen kisses she pressed on him. She also kissed Heather and gave Margot a squeeze as well for good measure.

"Lovely to meet Heather's mother," Aunt Jean said. Bill caught the blush on Heather's cheeks and the look of pleasure she could not fully hide.

When he finally disentangled himself, he called Tribal Rangers and told them where they were headed and why. They promised to send a unit to check on things when they could and run a search on Egan. He loaded the ladies up in the truck, leaving Tank with Aunt Jean just in case.

They bumped along until they came as close as they could and then continued slowly on foot, with Heather holding on to her mother's arm, supporting her when the ground became uneven.

"So you're not going to tell us what this treasure is Egan is after?" Bill said.

"I wouldn't want to get your hopes up if I'm wrong."

"Are you wrong?" he said.

She gave him a sly smile. "Not usually."

He sighed as they continued, glad that the morning temperature was still tolerable, the trail unwinding beneath them.

Heather pointed to the gorge to their left. "That's the dividing line between this property and Charlie's, I think."

"So we're officially trespassing now," Margot said, a cheerful smile on her face.

Bill chuckled. "Your mother has become quite the rebel."

Heather smiled. "Trouble, just like her daughter."

He couldn't argue with that. "The guy on the motorbike was rounding this bend," Bill said as they passed a sharp turn. The cliff walls rose up on one side, sharp and stately. Past the turn in the distance rose a hill covered in brush with exposed patches of yellow earth poking through, like scalp through pockets of thinning hair.

Margot took out her binoculars and trained them across the hillside. "There," she said, stabbing a finger at a spot just below the midline. "That's it."

She handed Bill the binoculars. He squinted until his eyes burned. "What? I don't see anything but bushes and a bleached-out log." He handed the binoculars to Heather.

Margot laughed, sounding like a much younger girl. "That's not a log, Mr. Cloudman. It's a fossilized bone. More specifically, the bone of a woolly mammoth."

Heather would never have been able to identify it without help. In disbelief she found the spot her mother pointed out.

"You see, this area was a sinkhole," Margot said, "probably formed when an underground spring dissolved an underlying layer of limestone, causing it to cave in. Eventually it filled with water. This used to be a much different climate, remember. Mammoths came to drink here, but once they got in, they couldn't get out. They were trapped and eventually became fossilized, invisible until the surrounding shale ultimately eroded and exposed the fossils."

Heather finally found her voice. "Fossils plural? More than one?"

"My guess is there is more than one perfectly preserved mammoth skeleton in there waiting to be excavated. Such a find is worth millions, and the prestige of owning and excavating such a find is incalculable."

"Exactly." Egan's voice started them all.

They whirled around to find Dr. Egan standing there, sweat stained and disheveled, a gun in his hand. "I'm not happy to find you all here at the site of my treasure, but I feared you'd figure it out sooner or later."

Bill put his hand on his own gun, but Heather saw him stop when Egan trained his weapon on her. "Please don't do anything rash. I really don't want to kill anyone. There's been too much killing already. The whole thing has gotten completely out of hand." His voice quavered as he spoke.

Her heart jumped to her throat. The sight of him there with a gun in his hand was so unexpected. "Did you shoot Oscar?"

"I had to. He was crazy." Egan shoved his glasses up on

his nose, words spilling out of him like bats from a cave. "I had to protect my fossils."

Bill spoke quietly and Heather realized he was trying to buy time, to calm Egan down. "How did you discover this spot, Dr. Egan?"

"I hired Leanne to show me around when I first came." He gestured to Heather. "Your property was vacant, so we hiked here and I spotted this from a distance. Leanne didn't have a clue what she was looking at. A priceless, breathtaking find right here under everyone's noses. Unfortunately, when I went back later, Oscar saw me and he wasn't about to be put off. I had to cut him in or he'd go to Charlie. I paid him to keep an eye on the property. Leanne must have figured out that I had an interest in the area for some reason, because she went back on her own to look around and Oscar killed her, stupid fool."

Heather saw Bill's jaw tighten. His fingers moved toward his gun, but Egan seemed not to notice.

"What then?" Bill said, voice tight. "What next?"

"Later Oscar told me his wife figured out what he'd done and he had to kill her, too. It just disintegrated from there." Egan was sweating heavily, his face unnaturally flushed. "I was going to buy Charlie Moon's land. I told him there was uranium contamination and no one else would want it. I told him not to tell anyone or he'd have to pay for a cleanup. He agreed, of course, but his nephew suspected something was up."

Heather gasped. "Johnny suspected someone was pressuring his uncle to sell?"

"Yes. That's when it all started to unravel."

Bill's voice was low and deadly. "Did you help Oscar hide from us after he killed Hazel?"

"I gave him some money. I had to. I was in too deep. Oscar figured he'd wait for you to find him and use the opportunity

to kill Johnny, which would keep my land purchase on track."
Egan looked at Bill. "I think he meant to kill you both, of
course, but it didn't work out. Oscar was a filthy murderer,
too concerned with the small details to see the big picture."

Heather could not believe what she was hearing. So many
deaths. So many lives wasted for a pile of ancient bones. She
felt suddenly angry. "What about you? You killed Oscar because you figured he would rat you out if he was captured."

"You should have done that," Egan shouted to Bill. "You
had your chance down there at that construction site and
you didn't kill him. I figured if you saw the setup you could
stage an ambush or something. That would have solved everything."

"Then why did you call and tell Oscar that Bill was at the
warehouse? That was you, wasn't it?" Heather asked.

"I needed it to be over. I knew Oscar was going to use you
to get to Bill and if it didn't work, the plan could go on for
weeks. By that time, someone might stumble onto my find. I
had to force a confrontation."

Her mind boggled. "You're a professor and you're talking
about lives here."

"Yes," Bill snapped. "Especially the lives of three women
whom Oscar nearly killed."

Egan waved the comment aside. "I'd have it, don't you see?
The greatest fossil find of the decade. That was the most important thing."

Bill moved so fast, Heather almost missed it. He drew his
gun and fired, catching Egan in the shoulder. Egan dropped
the gun and clutched his biceps, blood trickling between his
fingers. Bill was on him in a moment, and they went down in
a pile. The professor was no match for Bill, who turned him
over and twisted his hands behind his back, hissing in his
ear.

"Was your buried treasure really worth all those lives, Dr.

Egan? At least Charlie Moon will be able to profit from what is rightfully his."

Heather forced herself to breathe. It was over. Finally. A Tribal Ranger vehicle rolled up and two officers raced out to take Egan into custody. Margot looked out at the panorama. "Who would have ever thought it?" she murmured. "Right there, right under our noses indeed."

Heather walked over to Bill. He stood alone, watching Egan being tended by medics, who had arrived after the police. She wanted to touch him, but she was afraid. There had been so much disappointment heaped upon both of them. She remembered his words after they'd learned of Leanne's murder.

I'm not going to let anyone in, Heather. Ever again.

Her hand stretched out toward his shoulder until she heard him sigh, a broken sad sound that echoed through the warm air. She stopped and turned away.

Too much time had passed.

Too much hurt.

Too late.

Tears welled up in her eyes as she looked out onto the electric-blue sky and contrasting rust of the earth. They were the same parched cliffs and valleys she'd seen before, but now they did not hold the beauty she used to see.

Hands touched her shoulders and turned her around. Startled, she looked into Bill's eyes, gleaming jet-black. He opened his mouth and closed it again, looking away.

"What is it, Bill?"

He continued to stare at the blue sky. "I've never been good with words."

She wondered at the naked emotion on his face, and then it made sense. He was saying goodbye, for good this time. She bit her lip and willed herself not to cry. "It's okay. I understand."

He blinked. "I don't think you do. I was angry and scared

after Leanne died and I started to think the world was against me."

"Was? Did something change your mind?"

He sighed, and this time it was a peaceful sound. "I guess God reminded me that there are still plenty of people around who need forgiveness."

Her cheeks warmed. "Like me, for my drinking."

His hands stroked her shoulders, her neck. "No, like me for letting you go."

Her mouth dropped open. "But you tried…"

"Not really. I sent a few emails and called once or twice, mostly to assuage my guilt over arresting you. But I should have said…" He stopped for a moment and swallowed hard. "I should have said I love you, Heather. I know you've got problems and so do I, but I'll stick with you through it and we'll beat whatever we have to face together."

She could not control the tears then. "I can't believe you're saying this."

He tipped her chin up and kissed her deeply. She felt sheer joy scorching her insides, making trails through her soul.

"I should have said it long ago, but I was afraid to be hurt, afraid to lose someone else."

Her heart fluttered so strongly she wondered if he could hear it. "I don't know what to say," she whispered.

"Do you still love me? Or have I waited too long?"

She answered him with a kiss of her own, pouring all the longing and regret that she'd felt into it, until they both parted, breathless. Her heart beat with a new rhythm, a happy, vibrant song that trilled through mind and body.

How could she have found everything she needed here in this dry and dusty place? She caressed his cheek, checking to be sure what she'd just experienced was real. Tears welled up in her eyes. "Does this mean you'll have a chance to learn your way around that cookbook I gave you?"

He laughed and she thought she'd never heard such a wonderful sound. "Maybe so."

"What have you gotten through so far?"

He frowned in thought. "Let's see. I think I've managed to make my way through the table of contents."

Their laughter mingled. Heather looked over to see her mother watching her with a smile on her face, and she knew that there was no greater treasure in the world than what she had been given at that very moment.

She tilted her face to the sun and kissed him again.

* * * * *

Dear Reader,

I hope you have enjoyed this journey with Heather and Bill. Though they have both been grievously injured, they manage to come to terms with their pain and embrace the joy God has given them. We all have those wounds from people or circumstances in our past, don't we, dear reader? Forgiveness is excruciatingly difficult to give at times. It is far easier to hold on to anger and bitterness. My wish is that all of us can experience the true joy of God's forgiveness so that we can find our way closer to forgiving those who have wronged us.

Thank you for coming along with Bill and Heather on this journey through the Badlands. In the next book, Bill's niece, Kelly, will face her own struggle to survive in the harsh wilderness of South Dakota. She, too, will come face-to-face with past injuries and present dangers that threaten to overwhelm her. I hope you will come along for her adventure, as well.

I always appreciate hearing from readers. Please feel free to contact me via my website at www.danamentink.com.

Sincerely,

Dana Mentink

QUESTIONS FOR DISCUSSION

1. Heather believes that no matter where she goes she will never escape the pain of her mother's abandonment and her own bad choices. Have you ever felt that way? What is the antidote to this pain?

2. At one point, Heather makes the decision to leave South Dakota. How do you think her life would have turned out if she had left?

3. Heather realizes that the only way to heal is to make a choice "that will hurt deeply." Have you ever had to make a choice like that? What helped you through it?

4. Aunt Jean tells Bill that Heather will always be tangled around his heart. Who are some people in your life that you no longer see but who remain deeply embedded in your heart?

5. Heather struggles to accept Margot. What are the qualities that make someone a mother besides the physical act of giving birth?

6. Heather worries that if she leaves, she will be abandoning her family as her mother did. Do we sometimes make choices to consciously be like our parents, or deliberately choose to be different than they are? Can you identify the choices you've made?

7. Heather feels a mixture of fear, anger and resentment about her mother. How do you think God will help her deal with such emotions?

8. Margot says of her husband, "We were complete opposites and I loved him instantly." Which of Margot's qualities probably attracted Heather's father?

9. How did motherhood feel like a punishment to Margot?

10. As Margot points out, there is no rational reason why someone is compelled to love a person just because they gave birth to them. If God taught us how to love, why do we make such a mess of it sometimes?

11. Bill says, "I'm not going to let anyone in, Heather. Ever again." What other characters in the novel appear to have made the same decision? Do they change as the novel progresses?

12. Tank is a noble canine friend, as is Choo Choo. How does God use animals to bless us in our daily lives?

INSPIRATIONAL

Inspirational romances to warm your heart & soul.

SUSPENSE

TITLES AVAILABLE NEXT MONTH

Available September 13, 2011

LONE DEFENDER
Heroes for Hire
Shirlee McCoy

HIDDEN IN THE EVERGLADES
Guardians, Inc.
Margaret Daley

THE LAST TARGET
Christy Barritt

DEEP COVER
Undercover Cops
Sandra Orchard

LISCNM0811

REQUEST YOUR FREE BOOKS!

2 FREE RIVETING INSPIRATIONAL NOVELS
PLUS 2 FREE MYSTERY GIFTS

Love Inspired.
SUSPENSE